VLAD

THOSE THAT DON'T LEARN FROM THE PAST ARE DOOMED TO FACE IT.

STACEY ROURKE

"I have crossed oceans of time to find you."
                    -Bram Stoker (Dracula)

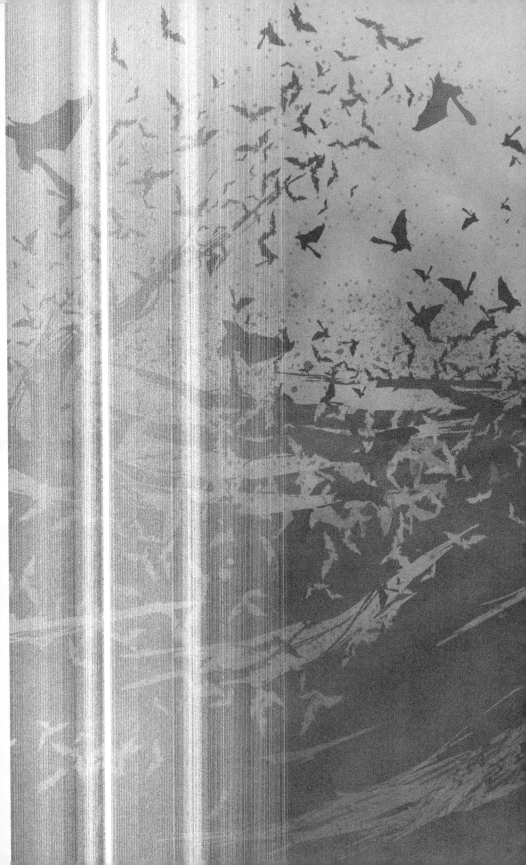

PROLOGUE

In blood I am called.
In blood I shall grow.
A worthy vessel chosen,
or … so the story goes.
Kneel at the altar,
Accept the sacrament on thy tongue.
Freely give thyself,
and stay forever young.
Life immortal shall be granted,
To those whose worth is measured.
Unlimited power placed,
in he who serves my pleasure.
Now and forever,
you and I could be one.
I'm in your veins,
in a bond that shan't be undone.
Fight, scream, struggle all you like,
I'm sorry to say, it won't amend your plight.
Reborn are ye now,
my first … child of the night."
--The Drákon

ONE
VLAD

I was ten years old when the darkness first spoke to me. Comprised of shadows, it roiled and stretched all around, taunting me with malicious hisses of laughter that reeked of fire and brimstone.

Barmaids carried steins full of frothy ale, weaving their way between tables of rowdy Hungarian soldiers. Fresh baked loaves were rushed from the kitchen's kiln to sate the hunger of men ravenous from weeks spent in the field. Tucked into the corner behind the kitchen's swinging door, I stood at a small spice table in the corner. Hands trembling, I dumped a vial of certain death into a pitcher of ale.

Beside me, Dorian Gray—the only friend I'd made since being ripped from my family—pulled a frog out of the sack dangling from his hip. Caramel complexion brightening with a gleefully rosy blush, he glanced my way with a toothy grin. Thick currents of ebony hair

1

waved from his scalp in every direction, gracing him with a crown of disarray.

"Now," he uttered under his breath, "for the incantation. *Καλώ τον πράκο*."

"*Dorian!*" Careful not to slosh the vial's contents, I elbowed him in the ribs. "*What, in the name of the Savior, are you thinking?* You can't bring such a filthy creature in here. It draws unnecessary attention to us. Put it away, at once."

Rolling his eyes, Dorian tossed a lazy grin my way. "If you want the magic, my little green friend is a key ingredient. That's how it works, *ο φίλος μου*."

"*I most definitely do not want magics!* The devil delights in such sinister practices." Feeling guilty by simple association, I jumped the instant the tavern's keeper burst in, spewing a stream of profanities about the tables that needed tending. I waited for him to storm back out before dropping my voice to an urgent whisper. "What I need is your help. I'm pouring out poison to a room full of armed soldiers! I beg you not to make me go in alone!"

"Remind me again *why* we were sent to deliver such a fatal brew?" Dorian countered, his eyebrows lifting in challenge. "Is it because you actually have a vendetta against the men out there singing loud and bawdy folk songs? Or, because someone else demands it of you?"

Glancing over my shoulder, I made sure none amongst the bustling kitchen staff were listening in. "You know the answer to that."

"*I do?*" Dorian faux gasped, clapping his free hand over his heart. "Oh, that's right! Because the mighty ruler, Sultan Murad II, *demands* it of us to ensure the stronghold of the Ottoman Empire. But, it doesn't *have* to be this way, Vlad! He's a cruel man who tore us— along with countless other children—from our families to prove his power and force them to bend the knee. Your own father, *the ruler of the principality of Wallachia*, had to *hand you over* to prove his obedience. Don't pretend you don't hate that just as much as I do."

"*I do!*" I spat, "But not enough to risk an act that could be perceived as paganism. The penalty for which is death!"

The sorrow of life caged in captivation sliced deep creases between Dorian's brows. "I've read all I could about this spell, from books children are never supposed to see. I can do this, Vlad, without us ever getting caught. It's simple, really. I utter the incantation, offer up the frog as a blood sacrifice, and *Drákon*—The Dragon—will be called forth. It will fill my vessel and grant me a strength so powerful we will never have to kneel before anyone again. Either of us. Think of it! We can stand against Murad!" Clapping a hand to my upper arm, he gave a firm squeeze of understanding. "We can go *home!*"

"That sounds glorious, indeed." Chewing on the inside of my cheek, I peered down at the tainted ale. "What if it doesn't work?"

"Well," Dorian's lips parted with a pop; as he spoke, he gently stroked the frog's head with the pad of his thumb, "that's the part where you carry on with Murad's plan to cover our asses."

"*Those steins aren't going to fill themselves, lads!*" the robust cook bellowed, wiping sweat from her brow with the back of her hand.

"*Da*, madam! We'll tend to the task, straight away." Snapping to attention, I collected the frothy pitcher between sweat dampened palms. I swallowed hard, then turned on my heel toward the swinging door that led out to the tavern area. There, I hesitated. "How long do you think you'll need?"

"Everything I've read about *Drákon* says that he comes swiftly once summoned, craving blood in tribute. So, the longer I stand here talking to you, the longer I wager it will take." With a formal roll of his wrist, he waved me toward the door.

"By all means, hurry." I managed through tightly gritted teeth.

Cradling the frog in his hands, he didn't waste another instant. Eyes closed, he whispered an inaudible chant against its back.

"*You!* Go, now!" The cook barked in my direction, shaking her wooden stirring spoon over her head.

Teeth chattering with fear, I pushed open the swinging door and stepped into the dining hall on quaking legs. Boisterous joy enveloped me. Soldiers sang off-color limericks at the top of their lungs. Laughter bounced off every wall. Some threw dice and gambled away a week's worth of earnings. Others, discussed their favorite scripture passages over a pint. Cautiously, I inched my way amongst them. I meant no ill-will for any among them, not that it mattered. If Murad's orders were not followed, I would suffer the cruelty of his hand once again. A fate I would wish on no man, woman, or child.

It was out of fear of that tyrant alone that caused my shaking hands to pour out one serving of ale, then another. With each glass I poured, every pint I topped off, I told myself I was doing these men a service. What I was offering would be a peaceful death. If left to Murad and his men, they would face days of anguish on the rack simply for the amusement of the Ottoman warriors.

Bumped by a stumbling soldier, I fumbled in a circle, careful not to spill what remained of my nectar of judgement.

"You do a service to us all," the bearded man slurred. Swiping the pitcher from my grasp, he slugged right from the rim.

My soul screamed for me to halt him, yet I knew doing so would raise a slew of questions that could easily cost me my life. Watching him glug it down, I said a silent prayer that his death be fast and painless. He was a man following orders, same as I. By the way he slammed what was left of the amber liquid, I guessed death would claim him quick. Letting the empty pitcher fall to his side, he wiped the drops of ale clinging to his beard away with the bend of his wrist. His lips smacked in appreciation. A blink later, he froze. Eyes bulging, his closed fist crushed against his chest. Dreading this was to be the pivotal moment that marked my soul forever as a sinner, my heart pounded against my ribs with a force that rattled bone. The man's jaw swung slack. It wasn't his last breath that stole from his lips but an impressive belch potent enough to make my eyes water.

"Another!" he roared, and slammed the emptied pitcher into my gut.

Brow furrowed, I sniffed the rim. Yellow Jasmine was lethal *if* administered properly. If diluted too much, the most the solution would accomplish was causing extreme drowsiness. I had been schooled on the proper technique, and warned of what to watch for. The quiet hush slowly steeling through the tavern was not a good sign. Nor were the yawns being hidden behind the backs of hands. Blinks were getting longer. One soldier's head fell to his chest. The abruptness of which jolted him awake with a snort. Knowing of my failure caused my back to tingle in fear of the lashes sure to come.

Tears blurring my vision, I hugged the pitcher to my chest. Knees locked in a straight legged gait of desperate determination, I bolted for the kitchen. Images flashed behind my eyes of the torment to come. To be sure, I would feel the unforgiving crack of Murad's whip. After he tired, his men would dump me on my cot in the bunk house. Unable to lie on my back, I would whimper into the thin mattress as my filleted flesh seeped and oozed.

So focused was I on the horror already playing out in my mind, that I didn't detect the threat coiling around me. A meaty hand clamped onto my shoulder, whirling me around. Stunned, I blinked up into the face of hate. A burly man—with one eye black as night and the other glacier blue—glared down at me. His lip curled into a malicious snarl, revealing teeth stained yellow with rot.

Snatching the pitcher from my grip, he brought it to his nose and sniffed. "Heavy on the hops, this brew. Yet, it holds a particularly … *floral* aroma."

"I---I merely poured the d-d-drinks, good s-sir," I stammered, gaze shifting toward the kitchen and the hope of escape.

Fist gripping the collar of my shirt, he yanked me closer. The reek of his foul breath caused my stomach to lurch in violent protest. "Is that right? This pitcher smells of jasmine, and my men suddenly seem ready to hunker down for the night. But you wouldn't know anything about that, now would ya, lad?"

Stare darting about, I hunted for a weapon in a room full of wooden plates and clay steins. "If you're displeased, I would gladly ask about it in the kitchen. Perhaps someone there will have answers—"

"You're not going anywhere," the man growled, jerking me back and forth hard enough to jostle my brain. "Someone told you to drug my men. I don't have to ask who. This type of underhanded act reeks of that Ottoman pig-fucker. What I want to know, is *why*? What's his play? And, I suggest you take special focus on the details."

Casting the pitcher aside, it bounced off the wall and shattered in a spray of shards. Hand freed, he drew a dagger from the sheath at his hip. He flipped it over the back of his calloused knuckles, letting it settle into his waiting palm. "Because the more I know, the less likely I am to skin you alive while all of these drunks watch."

Mouth opening and shutting, my body screamed for me to claim a breath around the lump of panic lodged in my throat. I had no way to know how things were progressing for Dorian in the kitchen at that same moment. I couldn't hear his chanting reaching a fevered pitch. Couldn't see his fist tightening around the body of the frog. Had I been privy to that crucial information, or understood what it meant, I would have let myself choke then and there. The sun has not set on a day since that I haven't wished that's how my story ended.

As it was, self-preservation brought on a bumbling fiasco for freedom. Lacing my fingers together, I arced my joined hands back and swung hard at the soldier's arm—once, twice, and again. With the final strike, he lost hold of me and the dagger. The blade skid across the floor, thumping against a neighboring chair. We dove for it in the same instant, my fingers beating his to be the first to close around its hilt. Knowing he could easily overpower me, I squeezed my eyes shut and blindly slashed in his direction. It sank into his thigh with a gruesome *pop*, chipping bone with the depth of the strike. Blood gushed from his leg in thick spurts, pooling at his feet.

With a slick of gore spreading across the floor, a chorus of gasps echoed through the tavern. The soldier's complexion grew paler with each second. A blue hue stealing over his lips, he sank to the floor.

I thought to run. Fast and far, and never look back. Had I tried, I would have found it already too late. Vines of darkness writhed through the tavern, stretching from the shadows. The candles strung overhead dimmed, flickering their subservient obedience. Could those around me sense the palpable presence of evil? I couldn't say. I can speak only of the shiver of unease that skittered down my spine, causing the hair on the back of my neck to rise.

The Dragon had been summoned, and in that pivotal moment I unintentionally supplied a worthy sacrifice. Choosing me as its vessel over Dorian, it slithered my way like a ravenous knot of serpents. They coiled around my ankles, twisting up my legs and torso. I stretched my neck as far as I could, head jerking side to side to keep them from my face. Lips parting, a choked sob escaped me as they snaked over my cheeks and wriggled into the corners of my eyes. A black haze blocked out the world, the taste of rotten eggs assaulting my tongue.

What followed was a haze of blood and violence. My dagger found its way through the room, delivering abrupt death without discrimination. Body moving of its own accord, I painted the walls with ruby spray.

From the darkest recesses of my mind came the rumble of a sinister voice, *Unlimited power placed, in he who serves my pleasure.*

I was ten years old when the darkness first spoke to me. Comprised of shadows, it roiled and stretched all around, taunting me with malicious hisses of laughter that reeked of fire and brimstone. In that moment, it called me … Slave.

TWO

VINX

Traveling in the private jet of an unnamed benefactor, we experienced mild turbulence flying over the Carpathian Mountains. Not that I noticed. Perched on the edge of a leather recliner, I stared without blinking at the TV fixed on the wall. A civil war was raging, gruesome images of hate and loathing strewn across the screen.

"To update our viewers on the current situation, a nationwide manhunt is underway for Rau Mihnea, the vampire activist who spear-headed the Nosferatu Presumption of Innocence Bill. Mihnea is wanted for questioning in the open investigation in the murder of Amber Rawling, daughter of Connecticut County Commissioner Lawrence Rawling. Video footage leaked to authorities appears to not only place Mihnea in the airplane hangar the body was found in, but implicate him in her death as well. We must warn those watching, that viewer discretion is advised as this footage contains graphic violence."

Blood-tinged tears blurred my vision as I watched the manipulated footage for what felt like the millionth time. Rau paced a slow circle around Amber and I. Blood seeping from my gut, I tried to keep myself between him and the frightened girl. He faked right, then darted left to weave passed me and claim his victim. On no channel were House of Representatives Member Alfonzo Markus, or County Coroner Neil Rutherford mentioned. The world remained oblivious to the fact that those two men drugged Rau with an artificial sulfur substitute that causes vampires to lose control of their hunger. Even if they tested his blood, they would find no trace of it once the effects wore off. Armed with that malicious weapon, the anti-Nosferatu activists were dosing vampires and sending them on violent rampages in order to build fear and unease among the human population. They wanted everyone to view us as monsters. It was working. The NPI Bill Rau had been fighting for, would have made vampires equal citizens in the United States. In light of all that transpired, it had been vetoed by emergency executive order. Across the country, violent protests broke out in metropolitan and urban areas alike, lighting the fuse for a string of vampire hate crimes. While cameras rolled, vamps were forced out into the sun, their attackers dancing and cheering as they burned.

Soft chanting lifting from the corner of the cabin was the only other sound to be heard. Elodie, a stead-fast follower of Rau, sat cross-legged on the floor. Her usual business casual attire, perfect for press conferences and photo ops, had been replaced by traditional Japanese hakama pants and a kimono robe knotted around her slender waist. Silky black hair was twisted on top of her head in a steel bun. Clutching an Order of the Dragon pendant—the official seal of Vlad Draculesti—between her thumbs and the bend of her index fingers, she pressed it to her forehead. Her humble prayer beseeched Vlad, the first vampire and god to our kind, to protect his people. Working side-by-side with Rau, she fought for acceptance and opportunities for the Nosferatu community. Now, much like the rest of us, all she could do was … pray. No doubt her prayers weren't exclusive for the vampire population, but also for her own battered heart. Her "brother" Thomas—a term used only because Rau sired them both—was piloting the jet after losing his hand protecting us during Markus's attack. The third in their "triplet" band, Duncan, gave his life for our cause only hours ago.

Hours?

Could that be right?

A collection of minutes, and everything changed.

One of the most pivotal differences being which side I stood on. I now proudly classified myself among the vampires. Something I thought I would never do. After watching my ex-boyfriend, Finn, slaughter my family, I made it my goal to expose the Nosferatu kind to the world as the monsters I believed them to be. Thanks to scientific advancements created by my parents, I was granted pseudo-vamp abilities in order to infiltrate their hives. All of their strength. None of their weaknesses. I should have been the perfect weapon against them … until I learned the truth. Even my own parents' death was a manipulation of the artificial sulfur compound. Can you blame the girl that is assaulted at a party after being roofied? No. By that same logic, I couldn't blame Finn for the part he played in my parents' death. Would I ever be able to look at him without wanting to slice the features off his face? Hell no. Even so, I accepted this matter was far bigger than him.

Unfortunately, the deceit didn't stop there.

As if spurred by my dreary thought, the picture on the screen changed. Markus's smug face, all toothy grin and coifed hair, appeared in high-def glory. "Since being hired on retainer by DG Enterprises, I have been privy to details of Rau Mihnea's countless violent rampages. All of which the vampire coalition paid to cover up. The most startling stories have come from his first victim, now *brave* enough to come forward."

Nostrils flaring, I dug my fingers into the armrests of my chair hard enough to puncture the leather.

"His story, of being held captive for over a year while enduring inhumane torture, is truly a heartbreaking one." Markus stared right into the camera without fear or hesitation, convinced his power and prestige would always protect him. "I ask you, can a being capable of such malevolence be called anything *except* a monster? My apologies, this isn't my tale to tell." Glancing to his left, he squeezed the hand of the person seated beside him. "Jeremy, the world is listening."

Memories of my brother having his neck snapped still haunted me, yet there he sat on national TV. Sandy blond hair falling into his warm chestnut eyes, he peered up from under his lashes to cast a lopsided grin at the camera. "I've told this story so many times now, I'm sure people are getting tired of hearing from me."

Scooting to the edge of his seat, Markus talked with his hands in animated gestures. "That's the problem exactly! We have to talk about this. We *need* to! People must hear the truth that lies at the heart of this matter. Too many vamp-lovers are idolizing anything with fangs, not realizing these serpents will strike the moment their latest food supply runs out!"

"Vinx?" A touch to my shoulder snapped my head around.

Without thinking, I dropped fang, my top lip curling from my teeth in a threatening snarl.

Retracting his hand, Carter Westerly raised them both in surrender. Despite the gesture, understanding roosted in the depths of his cerulean gaze. There was no denying the appeal of his charm and golden boy good looks. Unfortunately, Mr. Westerly once formed an addiction to the attentions of a female vamp. Fear of being nothing more than his next fix made *us* an impossibility. "Easy, killer. I come with word of Batdog, and Micah. And, yes, I purposely mentioned your pup first. I've learned that if you've got an ace up your sleeve, you play it."

Palming the remote, I turned off the television. "Where are they?"

Carter's hands dropped to his sides with a slap. The smile he forced came nowhere near reaching his eyes. "Micah grabbed the little guy before she and Finn hopped on their plane. They will be touching down in Romania within minutes of us."

Pushing off my chair, I leapt to my feet. "Look, I get why we jumped on this plane in the first place. A crazed maniac, willing to kill over his own jaded views, is a powerful motivator. But now, I think we need to take a beat. The Nosferatu and our allies are under attack in the US. Any chance of doing any real good is *there*. We're leaving the people that need us behind, to chase *Dracula*—a legend long since dead. We have a presence back in the states ... hell, we could take this to Congress, or any news crew that will listen! Back in the states, I can find Jeremy. I can talk to him before Markus gets his vile hooks wriggled into him even further. I could ..." voice cracking with emotion, razor blades of sorrow sliced through. "I could save him. I didn't get the chance to the first time. But, praise Vlad, I have a second chance. He's my brother. The only family I have left. I have to help him."

"Do not speak to me of losing brothers." Standing, Elodie planted herself in a pose of stone-cold conviction. "Duncan did not lay down his life that we may lose focus on what's truly important now. You speak of family, as if it were a simple concept defined only by genetics. Whether made in a lab, or sired, we are a member of the Nosferatu clan. Right now, *all* of us are under attack. If that means sacrificing a few to save the lives of many, that is what we will do. If we do not, our kind will be reduced to ash, ground under the boots of our enemies. Our only chance, young vampress, is to arm ourselves with the wisdom of the past." The grind of the jet's landing gear being lowered resonated like a battle cry answering Elodie's call to war. "To learn that lesson, we must journey to where it all began."

THREE
VLAD

I sat huddled in a corner with my knees to my chest. Slashes of blood covered my skin, and soaked my clothing. None of it my own. That sinister voice had quieted, leaving me alone with the horrors my own treacherous hands created.

Squatting beside me, his face ghost white, Dorian's chin quivered. "It was meant to possess me, but only for a moment. Never like this. By pulling that blade …" Eyes glassing over, his stare swept over the carnage. After a beat, he adamantly shook his head, denying my horrible truth. "All magic can be undone, transferred, or vanquished. Every book I've read says so. We simply have to find the proper technique. There must be a way."

Unable to gaze upon the massacre a moment longer, I stared instead at the dried blood on my hands. Caked under my fingernails, it stained crimson moons around my cuticles. "Take it away, or don't.

My soul is forever tainted by what happened today. Christ himself, would have me cast from Heaven into hells eternal fires."

"Maybe forgiveness could be found after countless acts of contrition?" Eyebrows disappearing in his hairline, Dorian peered up at the spray of gore that somehow managed to reach the ceiling. "And, a *whole lot* of Hail Marys."

"You're a devil." Crawling out from under the table she hid beneath, the cook crossed herself and glared daggers of hate in my direction.

Letting his head fall back against the wall, Dorian pretended not to notice the crimson ooze seeping into his hair. "Of course, there *are* two opinions on every matter."

"Spawn of Lucifer," she croaked, clenching the hem of her filthy apron in a white-knuckled grip. "Beastly, unclean ... *thing*! Ye'll burn for this! The wrath of God will strike ye down and *you shall burn*!"

"I think we've had our fill of that, wouldn't you say?" Filling his lungs to capacity, Dorian pushed off the floor. With a determined gait, he strode straight for the belligerent woman. "Be gone! Be gone with ya! We spared you once, we won't do it again! Run, or suffer our wrath same as the others!"

Tripping over her feet, she stumbled toward the door. Dorian continued his march, driving her back, until she escaped outside to be swallowed by the night.

Watching out of the corner of my eye, I begrudged his loyalty. Especially when I felt what I truly deserved was to be stoned. "You didn't have to do that. She was right. I will face judgment over what I've done. If not now, then soon."

"*Da*, sooner than either of us may like." Dorian stepped back from the door, obediently taking a knee and dropping his chin to his chest.

Knowing there to be only one reason for such an immediate reaction, I scrambled to mirror his subservient pose. I make no false claims of being a brave or valiant lad. My teeth chattered with a force that I thought was sure to shatter them the *instant* I heard the heavy footfalls of Murad's boots clomping across the planked wood floor.

He uttered not a word, but clasped his hands behind his back to tour the scene of hellish delight. Blood squishing beneath his feet, Murad maintained a steady, casual pace. Having completed a full lap of stepping over bodies, and jamming his sword into any he thought to be alive, he planted himself between Dorian and myself.

"The mission was to poison the Hungarian soldiers, that we may use their deaths to send a message to our enemies." His tone was melted gold--smooth and enchanting, yet undeniably deadly. "What do I find here instead?"

Risking a glance up, Dorian and I locked stares. Our brows furrowed with uncertainty over how to answer.

Lucky for us, Murad posed that as a hypothetical question. "What I found was a caliber of initiative not often found amongst men. Rarer still in young boys. Tell me, which of you orchestrated this attack?"

I thought for sure Dorian would point the finger at me. Not that I would blame him. While I didn't fully understand what came over me, I knew the punishment for it was mine alone to bear. To spare him having to turn on his only friend, I tipped my face up to Murad. Draped in gold-plated armor, he dragged one hand down the length of his beard. Every finger was bejeweled with precious stones, announcing his power and prestige to all those who gazed upon him. Mouth creaking open, I struggled to form the words that would undoubtedly seal my fate.

"*We both did!*" Dorian erupted. "T'was both of us, together, m'lord."

Murad's black eyes narrowed as he considered us. "While it's a far cry for two lads to achieve this level of carnage, it does seem it would border on *impossible* for one alone."

Outside, one of Murad's men accompanying him gagged over the tavern's grisly display.

"My question," Murad continued, twisting the ring on his pinky finger, "is *who* formed the plan that was carried out here?"

"As he said, sir," I managed, loathing how my voice cracked, "T'was both of us. Equal contributions led us here."

17

It wasn't a lie. Not really. Had Dorian not called forth the Dragon I wouldn't have fell victim to its influence.

Holding his arms over his chest, Murad's armor clanged together. "On top of everything, they believe in the strength of brotherhood." Shaking his head, gray streaked hair brushed his shoulders. "Many called me mad, and doubted my methods, when I brought children into the folds of war. Behold what has grown from my efforts: a pair of cherub-faced lads deadlier than any blade." With a crisp turn on his heel, he strode toward the door without a glance back. "The message here is clearly written. We need only ensure it is seen. Set a fire outside. Let's draw a crowd to this spectacle."

"And the lads, sire?" One among his men ventured.

Glancing back over his shoulder, a wry smile curled across Murad's narrow face. "Them? They're coming with us, of course. The finest room within my court shall be prepared. Any luxury they desire, that is within my grasp, will be granted to these industrious young men. From this point on, they are protected under my command, and considered an intricate part of my army. Anyone who dares to challenge, or harm them in any way will answer to *me*."

Somewhere deep within me, the Dragon hissed its wicked glee.

FOUR

VINX

Stepping off the jet, the wind lashed my hair against my cheeks, tossing what should have been my sleek bob haircut into a tangled disarray. Heavy gray clouds blocked out any traces of the sun, granting a temporary reprieve for the true vampires. For the moment, they could venture out without blanketed cover or the bothersome fear of spontaneously bursting into flames.

The second the soles of my shoes connected with the concrete runway, I was greeted by a merry symphony of excited yips. Batdog, the French Bulldog I rescued from one of Markus's twisted associates, wriggled free from Finn's arms and scampered straight for me as fast as his chubby little legs would allow. Pointed ears blew back as he ran, and his tongue slapped against the side of his face. Happily scooping him up, I squeezed my eyes shut while he covered my face with sloppy kisses.

Carter reached over my arm, to scratch the pup's adorable smoosh face. "Oh, sure, when Batdog greets you like that, it's cute. When I do it, I get told I should never have a third margarita."

"If it had just been *me* you did that to, it would have been okay," I jabbed back, shifting the wriggling pooch from one hip to the other. "Don't pretend you don't know that's why the mail lady doesn't ring the bell when she drops off packages anymore."

Our attempt at lighthearted humor was squashed when we caught a glimpse of Micah rounding the nose of the jet. Head hanging, her long rope braids fell in a curtain that shielded her face. Arms crossed firmly over her chest, even at twenty yards away I could hear her sniffles. Tears slipped from her lashes in a steady current, glistening zigzagged paths down her mocha cheeks.

Finn hung back at a respectful distance for a beat before hesitantly following her over. Maintaining an arms distance space, his silver-blue eyes traveled the length of her. Seductively handsome with an edge of danger, he dripped with sexual charisma. Undeniable pretty packaging—unless that package tore your family to pieces. Combine that with his arrogant demeanor, and tolerating him without bloodshed was the closest we would ever get toward reconciliation.

"Mics?" Carter ventured, taking a tentative step in her direction.

Micah wiped her nose on the back of her hand, her almond-shaped eyes brimming with blood-tinged tears. "I ... I didn't know," she managed, chin quivering with a fresh round of sobs.

"Know what?" My gaze lobbed from her to Finn and back again.

"Jeremy!" Her voice broke at his name, shoulders shaking with a fresh peal of sobs. "I had no idea he was alive. The officers on the scene ... my field techs ... all confirmed you were the only survivor. Had I known, I would have brought him to the facility. I would have done all I could to save you both."

"She's been crying since she saw the footage." Looping his thumbs in the front pockets of his black jeans, Finn's shoulders rose and fell in a shrug of indifference. "I tried to tell her I was at that house and the kid even *smelled* dead, but that didn't make her feel any better."

Carter pantomimed a stunned jerk at that revelation. "Wait, that *didn't* make her feel better? Weird. It's almost as if she can't find the humor in the death of a sixteen-year-old kid."

Setting Batdog down, I let him run sprints around our cluster while I closed the distance between Micah and I. Rubbing my hands up and down her arms, I searched my brain for some sentiment that could make any of this better. Finding no such thing existed, I settled for the ugly truth. "I watched them break his neck, Mics," I managed, in little more than a raspy whisper. "That bottom-feeder vamp I killed told me he drained what little life was left in Jer, then took his ear as a trophy. How he could have survived any of that, I don't know. There's no explanation for it, nor should you blame yourself in any way."

"Actually, Miss Larow, I can think of one very simple explanation you failed to consider." They moved in a silent flock, riding the wind with little more than the rustle of fabric. Their team was made up of nearly twenty, comprised of men and women. Practically every race imaginable was represented amongst their numbers. All had their heads shaved, and wore matching black smocks and coordinating pants adorned with red piping. Broadswords, nestled in supple leather sheaths, were slung across their backs. The hilt of each engraved with the symbol for the Order of the Dragon.

It was a black man with an easy smile, in the middle of the pack, that spoke. Pausing, he sent a nod of recognition to Elodie as she trotted down the stairs of the jet with her bag flung over her shoulder. "I would guess your brother either had the serum your parents' created in his blood stream prior to his death, or he drank from a vamp shortly beforehand."

I could feel the ache of my threatening fangs, and straightened my spine in attempt to keep my brewing rage contained. "My parents, whoever the hell you are—" Seeing his mouth swing open to fill in that blank, I held up one finger to halt him. "Not asking, don't care. Point is, they kept their work on that project far from my brother and I. They *never* would have experimented on us without us knowing."

mile widening, his gaze sharpened with equal parts interest and amusement. "I never said it was them, nor did I say he didn't know."

A slew of nasty expletives threatening, I dragged my tongue over my top teeth. "Look, Captain Asshat—"

"He goes by Ego," Elodie interjected. Striding into the heart of our huddle, she punched her bag into Finn's gut for him to take it. "He's a member of the V.H.M."

"Oh, shit!" Micah snorted, laughing through her tears. "Vinx went for the passing insult. Elodie opted for the roundhouse-nut punch combo!"

Clapping her fist over her heart, Elodie offered the squadron a salute they returned. "No one's nuts were punched, I assure you. These elite humans are members of the Van Helsing Magi. Sworn protectors of Lord Draculesti. Guardians of the Nosferatu way of life. Once joining the ranks, they forego their identity and take on the full name of the mortal sin they are most guilty of. As you can see by his smirk, Ego has yet to overcome his earthly curse."

Ego's smile vanished, wiped away by a locked-jaw scowl. "Last I heard, you no longer have a place here, Elodie. You serve Vlad's traitorous son, Rau Mihnea now."

A pale magi, with delicate features and a dusting of orange freckles across the tops of her cheeks, nodded her agreement. "It was our understanding that your position as a Court liaison had been revoked."

At the belly of the jet, the ramp service agents began unloading the bags from cargo. A heavy-set member of the crew, with a scruffy beard morphing into the rolls of his chins, scoffed in our direction. "Fucking fangers," he grumbled.

No one needed vampire hearing to catch his derogatory utterings, yet none among us reacted--so familiar were we with that type of narrowminded thinking.

"Really, Rage?" Ducking out from under the rounded jet doorway, Thomas pulled himself up to full height. "Tell me, would her loyalties, or mine, have been questioned in the slightest had it been known that we were following orders assigned by Renfield,

Vlad's oldest living ally?" Considering he kept his sandy blond hair buzzed short and maintained a rippling physique, he could easily pass for a member of the troop standing before us in their matching jammies.

"Why should we handle their luggage? Not like we're their servants!" Face reddening, the ramp agent pulled a black samsonite suitcase from the bowels of the jet, and frisbeed it onto the luggage trolley.

"How about, because it's your *job*, Phil," his gangly counterpart—a man all limbs and nose—lobbed back without glancing up from unloading the plane.

The suitcase Phil threw slammed into the back of the trolley, and the lid popped open. Out spilled Elodie's designer duds, and drool-worthy shoes. While the others seemed content to continue ignoring the man's rants, I was developing an anxious twitch behind my right eye.

"Brother Thomas, we were not aware you were here." Pure gristle beneath his uniform, a magi of Asian descent drummed his fingers against the sheathed blade resting at his hip. "However, this changes nothing. Renfield mentioned no *special* missions."

"I couldn't let Elodie have all of the fun here, now could I, Idle?" Thomas rubbed the palm of his good hand over the stump of his severed appendage, chest puffed in challenge.

Rocking back on his heels, Carter combed one hand through his hair. "Ego, Rage, and Idle? Add Sleezy and Pyro to the mix and you've got the lesser known cousins of the Seven Dwarves."

"Be quiet, or I will quiet you," Elodie mumbled out of the corner of her mouth, not in threat but absolute certainty.

Behind us, ole Phil's tirade escalated. Planting his feet, he jabbed his sausage fingers in the direction of Elodie's splayed belongings. "Look at this! I work two jobs to feed my family, and this undead bitch is draped in Gucci?"

The tendons of Ego's neck bulged, hinting Phil's commentary wasn't going as unnoticed as I previously thought. Even so, duty and honor kept him focused. "If you truly were on assignment, why would you abort that to come back now?"

"Phil, quiet down," the other ramp service agent mumbled, purposely keeping his head down.

"The hell I will!" Fed by his hatred, Phil's complexion bloomed from red to purple. "I've seen the news; people burning these unholy demons in the street! I say that's a good damned start!"

Maybe I was speaking out of turn, but in that moment, I didn't care. Hate is an ugly beast of ignorance that often shrinks when confronted. "*This* is exactly why we're here." I stabbed my thumb in Phil's direction. "Our kind are being targeted by *this* level of narrow-minded loathing. It's an epidemic spreading across the United States that's heading this way. If we let that happen, *none* of us are safe."

"You got something to say to me, *bitch*?" Phil spat. Nostrils flaring, spittle foamed at the corners of his mouth like a charging buffalo.

The chill of Elodie's cool flesh brushed mine as she elbowed me. "Ignore him."

"No," the cute little pixie they called Rage refuted with a wag of her finger. "We've heard all about this artificial vamp. It seems if she—or any of you—truly want access within our compound, proof of loyalty is required."

"W-what does that mean?" I whispered to my people behind my hand.

"I'm waiting, slut!"

"In a minute, *Phil.*" I snapped before turning with lifted brows to absorb Elodie's guidance.

"It means," Elodie's nose crinkled, as if the words soured on her tongue, "they are trusting you to … *handle* this matter."

"Like … *handle* it?" I mumbled, dragging one finger across my throat in a slicing motion.

Elodie blinked in my direction, struggling to decipher my moronic frequency. "Yes, because *that's* the kind of scandal we need right now. Or, if we *aren't* trying to add fuel to the fire, you can crush him *without* laying hand or fang on him. I watched some of your interviews. I know you have it in you."

24

"Aw, you watched?" I feigned bashfulness for a half a second, then squared my shoulders and spun in Phil's direction. "Don't worry about this little piss ant. I've got this."

"Artie, turn your camera on! Record this!" Phil demanded, swatting at the air between them.

Stretching out his hunched back, Artie reluctantly reached into his back pocket for his phone. "Man, I really want no part of this." Nevertheless, he thumbed the device to life.

"We need to capture every moment! Knowledge is the only protection we have against these bloodsuckers!" Hands curling into fat little fists at his sides, Phil's confrontational glare met mine.

Lacing my fingers, I let my hands fall in front of me. "Is that a fact? You know this because vampires harmed you or someone close to you?"

"Fuck no," Phil snorted, "Me and mine are smart enough to steer clear of you filthy devils."

"I see," I nodded, casting a knowing glance to the camera. "May I ask, what source are you drawing the information from that we mean you any harm at all?"

"I seen the footage of that fanger who killed that girl!" Phil stabbed his index finger in my direction, as if I were to blame for the attack. "Your truth is out there for the entire world to see! It won't be long now until you're *all* toasted nice and crispy."

"One death reflects on our entire species?" I asked, head listing with interest.

Pivoting his upper body, Phil yelled into the camera. "Hell yes! Shows them all for the monsters you are!"

Shifting my weight from one foot to the other, I wet my lips and readied for the KO combo. "John Wayne Gacy. Ted Bundy. Jeffrey Dahmer. All humans, all vicious serial killers. By your own terms, their actions would define every person with a pulse as monstrous and demented. Wouldn't you agree in the falsehood of such a broad generalization?"

"I don't agree with *shit*, you undead whore." Beads of sweat dotted his pudgy forehead, white foam gathering in the corners of his mouth. "What about all those other attacks playin' on every channel? Crazed vamps tearing into crowds of people!"

That verbal uppercut landed. Shaking it off, I fought to keep my expression cool. "Attacking the same people that are dragging our kind into the sunlight, and burning our camps. By no means am I saying it's right. However. cornered animals of any kind are prone to strike."

"That's just what you are!" Phil steamed. Stepping closer, his rank breath reeked of cabbage and halitosis. "An animal! Well, I'm calling you out right now!" His palms connected with my shoulders in a rough shove. "What are you going to do about it? *Huh*?" Shove. "You going to lose control, demon bitch? Show us what you really are?"

Before he could lay hands on me again, I dropped fang.

Artie gasped.

Phil froze, a victorious gleam narrowing his beady eyes.

Elodie started over, only to be halted by Micah's extended arm.

Locking stares with the narrow-minded bigot, I let my tongue tease over the tip of one fang. "If I was *ever* going to lose control, it would take a hell of a lot more than some miserable little nobody like you. I don't know what your problem is. Maybe your mommy and daddy didn't hug you enough. Maybe the neighbor used to touch you in a no-no spot. I won't claim to know your damage. What I *do* know, is that one of us just showed their ugly truth to the world, and it wasn't me. So, go ahead and post that video everywhere. Let it go viral. Then, each night, when you're laying on your soiled mattress, I want you to the think about the fact that you announced yourself as an *enemy* to the things that go bump in the night. Every branch that scratches against your window pane, every shadow that stretches across your floor, you'll lay there and wonder if you're *truly* alone. Sleep tight, asshole."

I didn't wait for his response, but turned on my heal to march back and plant myself in front of the magi.

In my wake, Phil eked out a plea, "Artie? *Ahem* ... erase the video."

The collective mood within the huddle shifted, each magi considering me with appreciation.

Turning my head in one direction then the other, I let my gaze wander over each of them before uttering a word. "Enemies of the Nosferatu are rising against us, armed with weapons this world has never seen. They are hell-bent on bringing about our extinction. As sworn protectors of our order, it seems unlikely you would be shown any mercy. Our only hope, is to band together. *That* is why we have come. Whatever came before, whatever personal rivalries you're holding on to, I suggest you let them go. Because, as of this moment, all we have is each other."

FIVE
VLAD

I came to with my sword buried in the throat of a Hungarian soldier. Blood gurgled from beneath my blade, bubbling from the lips of my paling victim. Catching his slack weight, I lowered his body to the ground.

"Tis just a matter of bad luck, friend." Easing his head to the blood-soaked earth, I forced the words through my teeth. "Fate cast us on opposite sides of this war. Go with God, fellow brother in arms."

A final breath rattling from his lungs, the soldier's eyes rolled back.

Eight years.

That is how long it had been since The Dragon snaked its way into my soul.

Whenever it took hold, I was forced down, buried within my own mind. Only when its pull lessened would I awake in the midst

29

of some gruesome assault inflicted at my hand. Every encounter was unique, each more grisly than the last. One element could be counted on; The Dragon *always* granted me a glimpse of our latest atrocity. I was its puppet, yet the beast never missed the chance to remind me I could become so much more.

On the heels of every blackout, that unholy hiss would echo through my mind, its devilish intent sending a shiver down my spine. *I am the demon Drákon, born in the depths of hell by my father, Lucifer. Drink of the blood of your victim in sacrament to me. Only then will I bestow the unlimited gift of* true *immortality. Power you cannot imagine. Strength no man can match. No longer will you fade into the darkness, but rule over it. Drink, my child. Drink, and live ... forever.*

I wish I could say that the thought repulsed me.

That my stomach churned at the loathsome idea.

Such words would taste a lie on my tongue.

In spite of myself and my every belief, my gaze tugged to the trail of crimson pooled around the cooling corpse. Smelling its coppery aroma wafting through the air, I dragged my tongue over parched lips. Every cell in my body sang out for a simple taste. Just a nip. Surely all couldn't be lost if I indulged in a sampling of the nectar of life.

Yes, yes, The Dragon purred, sensing my weakening resolve. *Bond yourself to me ... until the very end of days.*

It was my hatred for that repulsive curse that granted me the strength required to step away. Sheathing my sword, I kept my gaze fixed on the dirt beneath my boots in my march to the edge of the camp where my steed was tied. While I had moved in under the shadow of night, the cresting light of dawn now revealed all that transpired. Bodies impaled on their own swords. Charred remains stalled in frantic crawls from burning tents. Not one that stood against me remained. They never did. The only thing that made this bout different from the last was the stitch in my right side. Gingerly touching the tender spot, I found a gouge sliced through my armor to the flesh beneath. Someone got a lucky swipe in. No doubt The Dragon made them pay for it in torturous fashion. Poor bastard.

Garreg, my gray Shire stallion, snorted and tossed his head as I neared. Flipping his platinum mane, he protested the noisy clang of my armor. I clucked my tongue against the roof of my mouth, steadying him with a comforting hand to his muzzle. All I hath wrought, and he didn't shy from my touch. What other being on Earth could be so understanding? Gathering my reins in one hand, I slid a boot into the stir-up and heaved myself into the saddle. Settling onto the supple leather, I clicked to Garreg and tugged him to the north, back in the direction or Murad's dominion. A nudge to his sides with the heels of my boots, and he launched into a smooth canter that never bounced me from my seat. A mercy I was thankful for with my oozing wound. Wind lashing against my cheeks, I cast my stare to the looming horizon and pleaded to God for forgiveness … once again.

COURT HAD STILLED for the night. No longer did people mill about for the sole purpose of being seen in their most regal attire. Peddlers had packed away their wares, eager for a fresh rash of sales come morning. In mere hours they would fill the square once more, set for another day of extravagant spending. Those silent hours were when I found the castle grounds most appealing. Only then could I escape the binding fit of the role forced upon me. Murad spared no luxury when it came to his best warrior. Under that generosity, laid a harsh truth I was never allowed to forget: I was *his*. Murad's property. Little more than chattel, really. His whims were my decree. His fancy given greater importance than the air in my lungs. More times than I could count, I longed to escape. To my great regret, The Dragon had become accustomed to our lifestyle of violent indulgence. Any plan I concocted to claim my freedom was easily thwarted by yet another blackout. By body and soul, I remained trapped.

One small mercy to be thankful for; I wasn't alone. Pulling off my gauntlet gloves, I grasped the doorknob to my quarters and pushed open the door as quietly as I could. My care not to wake Dorian proved pointless the second I peered into our shared sitting room. He sat in the middle of the floor, a chalk pentagram drawn around him. Chin to his chest, a looping chant tumbled from his lips. None of that struck me as odd for him. What *was* slightly off-putting, was the barnyard stench that slapped me in the face the second I entered. In the corner, a goat merrily chomped on a bale of hay.

"Sakes alive, Dorian!" First checking to ensure no prying eyes got a glimpse of this spectacle, I slammed the door shut behind me. "Performing pagan rituals *openly*? Are you *trying* to meet the guillotine?"

Head tilting, Dorian considered me as if I were spouting gibberish. "We are in the lunar cycle of the Harvest Moon. That could be crucial for the success of the ritual. I waited up for you all night, but we need to hurry. The sacrifice must be made before the sun fully crests."

While Dorian had been a member of the guard as long as I, his body wasn't covered with the intricate tapestry of scars mine was. He blended with the distinguished men in the court who acquired their titles through clever political manipulations. In some ways, that was exactly what Dorian had done. He spun his talent for the dark arts into a vital position within the guard as alchemist to the men. They came knocking on our door in search of salves for whatever ailed them, believing him to be an expert with oils and herbs. Little did they know; spells and incantations were to thank for each and every one of his sought-after concoctions.

So many soldiers he helped, yet he failed me at every turn.

How many rituals had we attempted to free me from The Dragon?

How many moon cycles did we time our lives around in hopes that it would matter?

Each time, to no avail.

"The sun is almost up. It seems opportunity slipped through our fingers once more." Ducking out from under my breast plate, I shrugged off my armor and tossed it to the floor in a loud clang of metal. The gash in my side needed to be stitched, or at the very least cleaned. Be that as it may, my heavy blinks made either prospect seem daunting. "Maybe we could try again, in a day … or six."

"Not an option, my friend." Dorian scrambled to his feet. Catching my arm, he steered me back toward his circle. "If we miss this, we won't get another chance for a full year. Come, you can even sleep through it if you like. All that's required of you is to place your body next to the chalk line."

"You mean the chalk line of the protective circle I'm not allowed inside of, because it keeps you safe from the demon roosting within me? *That* line?"

"That would be the one, yes." Allowing me to sink to my knees in the designated area, Dorian scurried off to retrieve his wooden bowl and bundled sage from the wardrobe.

Catching my weight with one hand, I eased myself to the wood floor, eyes already clamping shut. "If laying down is all that is required of me, I may be able to accomplish that. I should warn you, though, I can't promise I won't bleed to death in the process."

Standing back to survey the lay out of his design, Dorian gently nudged the heel of my boot further from his safety circle. "I was going to ask if that was your blood, or someone else's. Either way, I think it could help us. *Drákon* does love frothy life by the bucketful. This could help us call him forth."

"Some of it is mine," I murmured. Rolling onto my back, my skull thumped against the ground. "Glad to know I'm bleeding out for the greater good."

Floor boards creaking under his feet, Dorian leaned over me to evaluate my injuries. "You're not dying. I can't even see bone. For an exalted champion, you fuss like a gassy infant."

"I swear, one day, you'll be the death of me, Dorian Gray." My attempt at a chuckle morphed into a hacking cough from the smoke I inhaled earlier that morning.

"Only if this goes *really* wrong." Situating himself in the center of the circle, Dorian sat cross-legged on the floor with his back board straight. One by one he lit the candles around him. The last of which he used to spark the sweet-smelling smoke of his bundled herbs.

Closing his eyes, he recited the summoning spell meant to call forth the unholy serpent within me. "*Drákon Enn Jedan tasa hoet naca Drákon. Drákon Enn Jedan tasa hoet naca Drákon.*"

Once, I made the mistake of chanting along with him. After speving blood out of every orifice of my face for a full day, I quickly came to realize this was *not* a crowd participation project. Instead, I filled my lungs to capacity, and waited for that tug that made my blood run cold.

Drákon didn't make us wait long.

He never did.

His essence trumpeted its arrival by seizing my muscles into taut ropes he could pluck at his pleasure. Choking on a scream, the taste of sulfur scorched my tongue. During a summoning he didn't force me under a blanket of darkness. I was made to watch him move and maneuver me like his own marionette meat suit.

Floating from the floor, The Dragon's grating voice—more beast than man—reverberated from my chest. "*You dare call forth Drákon?*"

"*Drákon*, I pay thee tribute with a humble offering." Dorian tugged the lead tied to the goat, pulling it to him.

Head tilted, *Drákon* smacked his lips in titillated interest.

Folding the goat tight to his side, Dorian flipped the dagger free from the sheath on his hip and drove it straight into the squirming animal's heart. Shushing its pained cries, he kept it locked under his arm in a deadly embrace until the thread of life severed. Swallowing hard most likely out of regret for what he had done, Dorian pushed the goat's body outside of the circle in offering.

Settling into a seated position, *Drákon* wriggled two fingers into the animals fatal wound. Extracting his hand, he held it up, watching the candlelight flicker off the crimson gore. "What is it you ask of me, human?"

Dorian rose to his knees, head bowed and arms thrown out wide. "By blood offering I pledge my devotion to you. Your current host is weary and unworthy. Allow me to be your vessel, that I may walk this earth in servitude to you and call you master."

The Dragon's neck rolled with a snake-like fluidity, eyes narrowing to lethal slits. "You speak of unworthiness, yet thought me simple enough to be swayed by a dead *goat?*"

Fingers curled into white-knuckled fists, Dorian let his hands fall to his sides. "T'was I that called you forth from the bowels of hell all those years ago. *I* was meant to be your host from the start. I've prepared for it."

The Dragon lunged forward, slamming against the invisible force of the protective circle. Bringing one hand to rest on its mystical barrier, he drummed his fingertip against it in a taunting tap. "You think my will is a sword I would ever allow *you* to wield? That you may use *my* strength to compensate for your deficiencies? You are nothing. An insignificant larva that would rather leach off my power than develop any of your own. I see you, Dorian Gray, for the languid coward you are. Kill a herd of goats, it will make no difference. I would sooner be vanquished from this earth than to ever allow *you* to serve me. Do not call on me again, boy. This circle cannot protect you forever."

Drákon's departure hurled me to the floor. Panting, I peered up at Dorian. "You okay?"

Grinding his teeth, he stared at the amber beams of light streaming in from the window. "The Hunter's Moon falls in the next lunar cycle. We'll try again then." Blowing out the candles, he gathered the tools of the ritual in his arms. "This isn't over. Far from it."

SIX
VINX

Proving even the undead can be moved by a good motivational speech, the V.H.M. extended us an invitation to Castle Dracul. Driving through the streets of Transylvania, I quickly discovered how skewed my impression of the land was thanks to Bram Stoker and Bella Lugosi. Wolves didn't chase our caravan of limos and Lincoln town cars. Heavy gray shadows didn't cloak the landscape in a foreboding gloom. Brides of Dracula didn't beckon wayward travelers into their lust-filled web of hunger.

Nope.

Not one of those stereotypes turned out to be true.

Damn it.

The reality was lush hills of rolling emerald, and cobblestone streets maintained with meticulous care. Busts of Vlad topped stone pedestals throughout the town, in honor of the man they viewed as a hero.

The castle swelled before us, a romantic vision of soaring towers and peaks of terracotta. Beside the manor sat an enchanting water fountain sculpted into the shape of a beautiful woman adorned in a gown of flowers. Pulling up in front of the grand estate, we found the beauty didn't stop at the arched walnut doors. The estate had recently undergone renovations to lovingly restore its original splendor. Polished wood floors were covered in exquisite antique rugs. Rustic beams ran the length of the soaring ceilings, adding a cozy feel to the castle's old-world elegance. Wrought iron chandeliers hung overhead, casting halos down on us commoners fortunate enough to stroll beneath them. Following the magi down a marble hall of grand archways and pillars, I began to think we stumbled into an *HGTV episode of Extreme Home Makeover: Castle Edition.*

That's when the creep factor finally caught up to us.

Ten cloaked figures, standing shoulder to shoulder in an ominous barricade, loomed at the end of the hall. Approaching on steps so smooth and silent they appeared to be floating, glowing red eyes gleamed from beneath the shadows of their black hoods.

Without a word, Elodie and Thomas separated themselves from the rest of our pack and ambled over to meet them. The ghostly figures glided around them, encircling the pair in what could only be described as a terrifying huddle of impending doom.

"Sh-should we help? Intervene in some way?" Micah leaned in to whisper.

Carter's mouth fell into a downward C as he adamantly shook his head. "They're what? A couple centuries old? I feel they had a good run."

Rising up on tiptoe, I craned my neck to see over the shoulder of one of the hooded beings. A pale and gnarled hand appeared from beneath a belled sleeve. Lifting it to their hidden mouth, the ghoulish entity bit down on their own frail wrist, causing two black pearls of blood to sprout from their skin. Without hesitation, Elodie mirrored the gesture. As the coppery scent of blood wafted through the hall, the two offered each other their wounds and drank deep.

"That ... is the grossest way to say hello ever." I grimaced in the awkward silence that followed.

Jerking as if slapped, the being holding Elodie's wrist recoiled.

"Is this true?" He didn't vocalize the question, but shouted it directly into our minds.

"God?" Carter asked the ceiling, eyebrows darting into his hairline.

Ignoring his interjection, Elodie dipped her chin in confirmation.

"The hour is at hand." The commanding boom reverberated through our skulls. *"Burn the candle. Call forth those who swear allegiance to Vlad. Tonight ... we wake our lord."*

DEAD WAS DEAD.

Despite being brought back from that eternal precipice myself, I still believed that. Pure blood Nosferatu were said to be immortal, yet they could be brought down by silver or sunshine. Therefore, I was skeptical, to say the least, that a vampire entombed for hundreds of years could possibly be resurrected.

The pomp and circumstance surrounding me argued otherwise.

A line formed inside of the Draculesti mausoleum, drawn there by four candles billowing inky black smoke out a window to the town square below. The magi were the first to claim their spot, followed by Transylvania natives, all eagerly willing to give of themselves to wake their savior. Each of the locals in attendance were adorned with a *Donator Tresâ*—a thin strip of black leather attached to a lone raven feather that was braided into their hair at the right temple. The accessory declared them supporters of Vlad, and willing blood donors.

Truth be told, I admired their faith. They believed with their whole hearts, while I felt life was an unforgiving sea of chaos that tossed and rolled us for its own amusement.

The eerie hooded beings, who Elodie explained were Nosferatu elders known as the Court, stood in a circle around a mosaic Order of the Dragon seal that decorated the floor. One by one they welcomed the next in line onto the seal, and offered them a pearl-handled dagger. With trembling hands, each volunteer dragged the blade down the length of their palm. Squeezing their hand in a fist, they let the sticky warmth rain down on the center of the seal in fat, wet splats. The crowd moved in a steady current. Slice. Bleed. On to the next. If any among them were getting impatient about the lack of activity coming from the grave below, they didn't let on. It's said that faith is a blind leap of hope. That day, it soared without abandon. Even when the steady stream of new arrivals began to thin, the faithful simply bowed their heads to pray for their lord to awaken.

"They all share the same dagger, yet no one has asked for it to be sanitized?" Micah observed, her nose crinkling in disgust. "I feel like we are watching the birth of a whole new thread of hepatitis."

"These are all faithful followers of Vlad," I murmured, glancing around at the white stone walls of the crypt. "They cleanse themselves by ingesting a drop of vampire blood each night. It's not enough to turn them, but keeps their blood healthy and pure. I learned that in one of the million books you made me read."

One corner of Micah's mouth tugged back in an almost grin. "And I thought you only paid attention to the ones with pictures."

"Not true. I started avoiding those after the trauma of the pop-up book."

"You. Your heart still beats." A grating voice stabbed into my brain, licking at the walls of my sanity. *"You will bleed, and He will rise."*

"What the hell, man?" Slapping a hand to my forehead, I checked to make sure my skull hadn't actually cracked open. "Give a little warning before the invasive mind probing!"

The hooded elder said nothing, but held the dagger out to me.

Before I could take a step, Micah's arm shot out to block me. "Correct me if I'm wrong, but in any and all bloodsharing ceremonies isn't it customary for the progeny to go before their sire?"

It was almost comical to watch those giant hoods turn to each other in search of clarification. A rash of nods spread through the lot of them, confirming Micah's claim.

Reaching for the hilt, her voice took on the cool, commanding tone of a college professor. "Her blood is chemically altered due to the manufactured version of her vampiric state. Mine is as well, but made marginally more organic by being sired by traditional methods. It seems a wise idea to try the lesser version on the vampire god before hitting him with a full dose. Wouldn't you agree?"

"Ever the scientist." Glancing down at that ominous seal, I chewed on my lower lip. "Quick question, oh brilliant one, are we sure a few drops of our high-octane advanced formula blood won't mutate whatever is in there into some sort of monstrous Uber vamp? Because that ... seems it would hurt our cause more than helping it."

Turning the dagger over in her grip, Micah's tongue toyed with the thin gold hoop in her lip. "I really want to say no. But, the thing about experiments is there is always an element of unpredictability." Gritting her teeth, she sliced into her palm. "Keeps things exciting, right?"

A heavy hush fell over the mausoleum as she closed her hand to let beads of life rain down.

Splat.

Splat.

Splat.

The floor shivered underfoot, barely noticeable to anyone not hyper focused on it. Which we all were. It was little more than a flutter, like the flap of a bat's wings launching it into flight. As suddenly as it began, it stilled.

"The other, now!"

"There's no time to waste!"

"Blood that he may rise!"

"The girl is the key! She must be!"

A chorus of voices pierced my frontal lobe, the anguish of their intrusion ripping a scream from my lungs. Folding in half, I pressed the heels of my hands to my temples, feeling that was all that prevented my head from exploding. "*Okay!* Shut up! I'll do it! But, before I do; one of you creepy SOBs shared blood with Elodie. You know all about me. Are we sure this is the way we want to wake up someone known as *The Impaler*? Seems he might not be the kind of dad you want to take unnecessary risks with."

This time they spoke as one, drilling their message deep. "*You will bleed, and He will rise.*"

"Good talk. I really feel heard," I jabbed back. Righting my posture, I accepted the offered dagger from Micah.

"Not too much. No more than a drop or two," Mics warned, her expression locked in a mask of concentration.

"Bleed, but not too much," I grumbled, weighing the blade in my hand. "It's always about the blood. Before my change I went entire days without thinking about it. I had hobbies, read books. Now it's all about ... the blood." Grinding my teeth together, I felt the bite of the blade against the meat of my palm. Scarlet drops fell on the head of the dragon, streaking between the tiles.

One drop.

Then, a second.

That's all it took to make the earth buck beneath me.

The walls shook.

Cement cracked with a thunderous boom.

Dust filled the air, blurring my vision and filling my lungs.

From within the pandemonium of destruction, he emerged. Features shriveled by decay, his jaws snapped in a vicious snarl. Before I could blink, he was on me. Knees catching my hips, he rode me to the ground. My head bounced off the floor with a sickening *thunk*. Black spots danced before my eyes. White hot pain radiated through me as his hooked fangs sank into my neck. Consciousness waning, I fell limp, powerless to stop the father of all Nosferatu from draining the life from me.

SEVEN

VLAD

For the first time since the rule of Suleiman the Magnificent, the Ottoman Empire has secured it's stronghold across southeastern Europe." Seated on his golden throne within the Ihlamur Palace of Istanbul, Murad combed one hand down the length of his beard. "That is thanks to the savagery and skill of this man, Vlad Tepes of House Draculesti."

A smattering of polite applause echoed through the throne room, twisting the ever-present knife of guilt deeper into my heart. "The credit doesn't belong to me alone, sire. It takes a powerful army to—"

"Now, now," Murad *tsk*ed, brushing his hands off on the front of his gold embroidered robe. For years he had hidden the gray in his hair with kohl, to maintain the illusion of his youthful virility. Fear of his wrath prevented anyone with an ounce of sense from mentioning the ring of dusky black forever encircling his neck, or the layer of soot that often covered everything he touched. "There is no need to be modest, young Dracul. The reputation you have earned has spread far and wide. Never have I witnessed a more ruthless specimen. Which is why I brought you here today. To reward your efforts."

Shifting my weight from one foot to the other, I gulped down the bitterness of his compliment. Every luxury bestowed on me, every compensation granted, further darkened my soul. "My life is but to serve, my liege," I muttered, respectfully bowing my head.

Thin lips twisting into a knowing smirk, Murad nodded to the guards stationed by the door. "As of this moment, that is no longer true."

Two of the guards strode to my side, their armor clapping with every motion. Unclasping the leather straps of my Ottoman crest breast plate, they let it fall to the floor with a deafening clang.

Brow furrowed, I glanced from them to Murad and back again.

"It is my decree," Murad boomed, throwing his arms out wide, "that from this day forth, you are released from the binding arrangement made between your father and myself. With my blessing, Vlad Tepes, you may go. The world awaits, *oğlan*."

Heart hammering against my ribs, I feared grabbing hold of that dreamscape would turn it to dust between my fingers. "My liege?" I managed.

Settling back against his bejeweled throne, Murad inspected his buffed and oiled fingernails. "You'll have decisions to make, of course. Where you'll go. What you'll do. The Dolmabahçe Palace sits vacant. Its gardens are the loveliest I've seen. If you were to settle there, we could find you a fitting bride to tie your bloodline with mine. My sister's husband is a worthless lay-about. Let me kill him for you. It would be my pleasure."

I could feel a threatening smile tugging at the corners of my mouth, brought on by hope and possibility. Lest my actions and demeanor be deemed inconsiderate, I battled to keep it at bay. "That is a kind offer, sire. However, if it's all the same to you, I would very much like to return home ... to Transylvania."

44

Murad clucked his tongue against the roof of his mouth, nose crinkling in distain. "That paltry burg? Why would you choose there, in light of all I could offer you?"

This time, there would be no suppressing my grin or the hot blush that filled my cheeks. "Why does any man commit any foolish act? There's ... a girl."

Resting his elbows on the arm rests of his throne, Murad's hands dangled over the rounded edges. "Of course there is!" His boisterous peal of laughter echoed through the hall. "Isn't there always? Other men struggle for a fraction of your military expertise. Yet you manage to juggle that, *and* find love. Tell me of this damsel whose hand you seek."

I had never spoken her name to another living soul, or confessed my feelings for her even to myself. Even so, with the path of possibility stretched out before me, my soul soared at the mere idea of it leading me straight to her. "She lives in my village. We used to play together when we were young. Her name is Jusztina, and her eyes are the color of a freshly sprouted meadow wet from a spring rain."

"*Hah*!" Murad threw is head back in another bark of laughter. "Such poetry! A tell-tale sign of that crushing first love. Tell me, young Dracul, does this maiden know of your affections and return them?"

So skilled was I with a sword, yet speaking of such matters made a hot blush seep up to my earlobes. "I ... believe so. We've exchanged letters through the years. She scents hers with lavender."

Clapping a hand over his heart, Murad feigned a pout. "Young love, I remember it well. So beautifully innocent. You simply must go to her, knowing if I ever call on thee again it will be your sworn duty to return."

Arm to my middle, I bent in a formal bow. "Without a moment's hesitation."

Murad dipped his head, rewarding my humility with a brief nod. "Then go forth, *oğlan*, and seek ye self that love eternal. If all else fails, you're always welcome to return. It would be my pleasure to kill my lay about brother-in-law for you at any time."

'I will send message straight away if the lovely Jusztina refuses me.' Feet itching to sprint from the castle, I risked a step back. "Sire, I must ask, what of Dorian?"

'Who?" Murad's face crinkled at the question.

The footman standing beside him, hands politely folded, leaned in to whisper in the high ruler's ear.

'Oh, *him*," he grumbled with a roll of his eyes. "He's a mediocre alchemist at best. I only tolerated him as a favor to you. By all means, take him with you as a parting gift."

'At your command, I will do so, and bid thee farewell."

'I bid! Go!" He waved me away with a flick of his wrist. "Leave my sight. I'm already bored of you. Go let love prevail, and all that nonsense."

Wide smile splitting my face, I needed no further invitation to sprint for the door. In her letters, Jusztina mentioned her father had been pressuring her to marry, since she was the last of her siblings to do so. If I could make it back before he found someone he deemed suitable, our love may yet stand a chance.

Boots scuffing over the floor, I mulled over what essentials I needed to grab from my quarters. Little more than the necessities were required. For freedom, I would gladly trade all the luxuries of my station.

Mind racing with what all I could fit in a satchel and still have room for canteens of water and provisions, I was oblivious to my surroundings until a hand hooked my upper arm and spun me around.

Face red with agitation, Dorian forced his words through tightly clenched teeth. "A castle? You turned down *a castle*? As a rule for life, when someone offers you *a castle*, you take it."

Clapping my hands to his shoulders, I gave him a supportive squeeze. "I feel like you're saying the word castle a lot, my friend, and, you needn't worry. We have no need for a borrowed castle when a whole glorious village awaits! We've been granted permission to retire to Transylvania!"

"You want me to go with you to your … farming community?" Dorian recoiled, shrugging off my touch.

"You don't know the thrill that awaits!" Turning on my heel, I resumed my stride down the open-air hall that led to the sleeping quarters. I held no doubt Dorian would fall into step behind me, if for no other reason than to continue yelling. "Working the land. Tending crops. It's man's work, Dorian! You will *love it*!"

"It's like you don't know me at all." He grimaced, following just as I predicted. "Here, we are exalted. Why would we voluntarily leave that?"

"Because, we don't need it!" I explained, throwing open the door to our quarters. "We have our freedom!"

Instead of following me inside, Dorian paused in the doorway. With his arms crossed over his chest, he leaned against its frame. "And what of The Dragon?"

Catching his wrist, I tugged him inside and shut the door. For added precaution, I dropped my voice to an urgent whisper. "This changes *nothing*. You want The Dragon? Take it. You can keep performing ritual after ritual to make that so. I would happily rid myself of its burden."

"Much appreciated, but not at all what I meant. The Dragon has kept us here because it *enjoys* our way of life, and the seemingly endless body count that accompanies it." Dorian's eyes narrowed to slits of warning. "What do you think will happen when you try to contain him in a sleepy little town full of innocent lives?"

"It doesn't overcome me as frequently as it used to. I can contain it, *and* manage a normal life. I know I can."

Oh, the lies we tell ourselves.

EIGHT

VINX

Sitting on the edge of the bathroom sink, I sucked air through my teeth at the prickles of pain awakened by Carter dabbing a wet washcloth to my neck. The puncture wounds from Vlad's sizeable fangs would have already healed, thanks to my upgraded cellular regeneration, had he not been wrestled off me by a small army of his own people. His locked jaws sawed through layers of flesh and tendon, leaving the magi with no choice but to lasso Vlad with silver chains to pry him off my slumped form. It took a full bag of blood and two of the pseudo-vamp serums to revive me, making it the second time in as many days that I had to be brought back from death's door. As budding hobbies went, this one wasn't the best.

Face folded in a deep frown, Carter wrung out the washcloth beneath the running tap, tinging the water a dirty copper shade.

Rewetting it, he resumed his delicate cleaning. "I have never felt more useless in my life. He had you pinned there, and I ... froze."

"You mean you *couldn't* single-handedly fend off the father of all vampires? What the hell am I even doing here, then? That's my only reason for hanging out with you." Catching his hand, I forced him to meet my eye. "Seriously, Carter, did you see how many people it took to pull him off me? Vampires *and* magi. I counted roughly thirteen before I lost the ability to decipher shapes."

Jaw tensed, he used the knuckle of his index finger to lift my chin. "That doesn't make me feel any better. He nearly ripped your damned head off."

White-washing my face of all emotion, I blinked in his direction. "Tell me the truth ... did he fuck up my hair? Because gushing throat wounds I can handle, jacked up hair I cannot."

With a bitter shake of his head, he swallowed down his boiling rage. "Can we please just ... for a minute."

I took the washcloth from his hand, folded it into a makeshift gauze, and slapped it to my neck. "You must mean business. There was a complete lack of verbage in that sentence. Sloppy work, Mr. Reporter."

Filling his lungs, Carter glanced my way, his handsome features marred by sorrow. "You're not the kind of girl who needs, or wants, to be saved. It would just make *me* feel better, if a situation ever got out of control, that I could ... you know."

"Verbs are not your strong suit, today." Scooting forward, I hopped off the edge of the white marble countertop.

Carter caught my wrist, and tugged me closer. "*Protect you.* All these life and death situations you're thrust into every day, and I feel powerless to keep you safe."

The warmth of his breath coursed over my cheeks, awakening a tinge of awareness in my core that his lips lingered mere inches from mine. Gazing into the luminous pools of his azure stare, I toyed with questions I was in no way prepared to answer.

"There are ways around that," a curt voice stated from the doorway.

Thankful for the interruption, I inserted a more comfortable distance between Carter and myself. Dragging my tongue over suddenly parched lips, I turned my attention to the petite frame in the doorway. "Rage, isn't it? We would *love* to hear some deep magi wisdom on this matter."

"Drink vampire blood," she stated flatly.

Nodding in hopes there was more, it took me a beat to figure out that she was done speaking. "Okay … not quite the opus of wisdom I was hoping for."

"You drink it, it makes you less of a wuss … for a while." One of the young magi's shoulders rose and fell with detached interest—her tone monotone and emotionless. "All members of the V.H.M. partake in this ritual daily to make us worthy to serve Vlad and his Court. Being stronger and more focused has helped me battle my mortal sin of blinding aggression."

Carter cleared his throat to hide his snort of laughter. "Oh … you're serious."

"If it wasn't for vamp blood, I would have ripped that towel bar off the wall and beat you with it for laughing at me." Rolling her shoulders, Rage straightened the hem of her shapeless black uniform. "But, here I am, rooted like an oak and not losing myself in the sweet release of a good violent outburst."

"Thank you?" Rapidly blinking my confusion, my voice rose just enough at the end to be a question.

Grabbing the actual gauze and medical tape off the counter, Carter replaced my makeshift bandage with the real thing. "As to the blood, it's not an option. I'm a recovering addict."

Rage lifted one brow, as if some early suspicion had been confirmed. "Gluttony in any form is one of the hardest sins to overcome, because it's rooted in weakness of the spirit."

"He's not weak." Catching Carter's stare, I held it firm while he fixed the last piece of tape in place. "Being surrounded by his addiction every day, without giving in, makes him one of the strongest people I know."

Filling her lungs, Rage expelled an exasperated sigh. "Then, I'm deeply sorry for your limited interaction with more substantial human beings."

"Can't lash out with her fists, but she can still hurt people with her words." Wadding up the wrapper from the gauze, Carter offered me a conspiratorial wink.

"I'm bored talking to you both, now." Rage grimaced. "Lord Vlad wants to speak with you. He's in the Grand Hall. It's down the right wing. Big hall, looks grand. You can't miss it." Offering no further explanation, she turned on the ball of her foot and strolled off in the opposite direction.

Head tilted, I watched her leave. "Cold. Abrasive. I don't know whether to hate her, or fall in love."

"You can swipe right on her later. Right now," he extended his arm in invitation for me to lead the way, "the king of the undead awaits."

Hand drifting to my bandaged neck, I swallowed back a lump of trepidation. "Let's hope it's not to finish what he started."

NINE

VINX

The throne room was silent as a grave.

Every head bowed with respect.

Against the farthest wall, sat a legend. Hand-carved from the trunk of a sequoia, the back of his throne swooped into two spikes that hinted at the Impaler's legacy. Gone was the bat-faced monstrosity that lunged for my throat, replaced by a man that radiated with power and prestige. His posture demanded respect. The coal black three-piece suit chosen for him painted him as a gentleman of means. An outsider may have guessed him to be nothing more than a successful business man, had he not been suckling at the wrist of a curly-haired woman wearing a *Donator Tresâ*. Retracting his fangs with a flick of his head, he dabbed at the corners of his mouth with a handkerchief, then handed it to his meal. She pressed the fabric to the puncture

53

wounds, and exchanged nods of acknowledgment with Vlad before backing from the room.

A wall of onyx capes loomed behind Vlad, every member of the Court standing at attention for their awakened king. The ruby gleam of their eyes scanned the room, sizing up the intentions of all who entered. Edging up next to Micah and Finn, Carter and I added ourselves to the mass of followers.

"Vincenza Larow, the first chemically manufactured vampire in creation." Vlad's voice was melted caramel over chilled ice cream. Lapping waves washing up on a white sand beach. A crackling fire on a crisp autumn night. Warm, inviting, and welcomingly seductive. "Though blood we of the original Nosferatu line are able to see through the eyes of others. When I drank of you, I saw the relationship you had with my son. One of kindness and caring. It pleases me to know he had people like you, and his triplets," a pointed glance to Elodie and Thomas, "in his life. I owe you my gratitude."

Lifting my chin, I addressed the vampiric god. "Your son is a good man. No thanks required."

"He was ... once." Vlad rubbed his palms together, intense gaze traveling the length of me. "I think we can agree your last encounter with him argues otherwise. In that vision, I understood your motivation to wake me. Tell me, this artificial sulfur injection, is it a real and viable threat?"

"My progeny and associate could speak on the effects," Catching Micah by the elbow, I guided her forward. "They were both injected against their will."

Propping his elbow on the armrest of his throne, Vlad motioned for Finn to speak with the wave of one finger.

"I live by your teachings, my Lord." Creases of regret bracketed the edges of Finn's down turned lips. "I feed on animals, or willing donors. But, the instant that concoction entered my system, I lost control. I killed without hesitation, and have regretted it every day since."

Vlad's shoulders sank, a deep V of concern puckering his forehead. "Many within the Nosferatu brethren need no special medications to suffer a similar loss of inhibitions. What of you, child?" Brilliant, sea-foam green eyes flicked in Micah's direction. "You were drugged, as well?"

"Yes, your honor. I mean … my Lord? Your majesty? Shit, I'm really nervous." Micah rambled, the tip of her tongue anxiously fiddling with the hoop in her lip. "I don't remember the details. I just remember an overwhelming hunger, and waking up covered in blood."

"I must reiterate, sire, that these are faithful followers of your wisdom." Good hand clasped over his heart, Thomas boldly spoke on their behalf. "They would do no harm intentionally."

Raising one hand, Vlad silenced further explanation. "That's quite enough. Like so many conflicts that have come before, this has escalated due to the nature of our desires. As long as there have been vampires, there has been a torch and pitchfork wielding crowd eager to destroy us. If we were free from the curse of our own ghoulish desires, they could not be used against us. Yet, here we are, once more. You should not have woken me for this. This battle will play throughout history time and again, until the humans finally succeed and wipe us from existence."

Head cocked, I peered at the man known as The Son of the Dragon. The physical similarities between he and Rau were easy to spot. They shared the same stature, narrow nose, and strong-jaw line. Unfortunately, it seemed that was where the family resemblance ended. Rau put himself at risk time and again to fight for his people, marching on Washington in search of equal rights. His father, on the other hand, couldn't be bothered to rise from his decorated seat of power.

"That's a bleak outlook," I lobbed back, forcing a tight smile. "We came here, because your people are being tortured and killed. They're living in fear. Knowing you're awake could offer them hope when they need it most."

"You came here," Vlad's tone sharpened with a dangerous edge, each word slicing to the bone, "in search of war. Lie to yourself all you like, I know the truth. You meant to unleash me on your enemies that I may exact your justice. I have played the part of weapon before, *copil*. I will not do it again, for anyone. I apologize for biting you without consent, Miss Larow, and your wasted trip here. You may have a day to rest and make your travel arrangements. Then, I want you gone. I will not have this pointless crusade brought to my door."

USHERED FROM THE throne room, Ego shut the door in our faces with an arrogant smirk twisting the corners of his lips. Fangs threatening, I spun on my team. "I liked that so-called Prince of Darkness a hell of a lot better when he was trying to rip my throat out. At least then he seemed to have a set of balls on him! Jeremy, Rau, and the entire Nosferatu population are suffering! Meanwhile, his royal lowness won't budge from his fancy ass chair!"

"Throne," Micah corrected.

"*Whatever*!" Throwing my hands up in exasperation, I paced the width of the hall. "Okay, it's like a math problem. We just need to work it to find the right solution. That's our thing, it's what we do. So, what's our move?"

"Kick Ego's teeth in?" Elodie's nostrils twitched her irritation. "I'll gladly volunteer."

"Let's call that Plan B," Thomas suggested, placing a calming hand on his sister's back. "Plan A needs to be getting Rau back. He always knows how to spin us out of nosedive situations."

"That's it!" I jabbed a finger Thomas's way, eyes bulging with possibility. "We need to think like Rau. Put ourselves in his head. What would *he* do?"

A beat of silence, then …

"He would find a way to get his hands on a vile of that sulfur." Arms crossed, Elodie chewed on the inside of her cheek.

Picking up the proverbial baton, Micah ran with it. "He wouldn't stop there. Without a doubt he would hold a press conference to expose it to the world, complete with controlled experiment footage of the effects of the drug."

Back to the wall, Carter crossed his feet at the ankles. "Let's not forget the guy's humanitarian efforts. I could see him arranging outreach programs for vamps and humans alike."

Palms turned up, the knot of tension in my shoulders lessened. "And, just like that, we have a plan. Elodie, reach out to the sponsors who donated to the refugee camps. See if you can line up emergency supplies. Micah, you've got friends in high places. We're going to need to secure a location. The jet needs to be gassed up and ready to fly as soon as the sun sets tomorrow. Thomas, I need you on that."

"The news stations are all me," Carter pushed off the wall with his shoulder, shoving his hands into the pockets of his slacks. "I can have a press conference lined up for the instant our wheels touch down back in the states."

"Fantastic." Pivoting on my heel, I pointed to Finn. "You—"

"I want to find Jeremy," he interrupted, the inflection of each word dripping with remorse.

Stunned by his request, a slight nod of encouragement was all I could muster.

"I'm with you," Micah linked her arm with mine. "We'll go check on Batdog, and prevent you from doing anything stupid—like storming back in there to challenge Big Daddy vamp to a fang-off."

"Bless you," I muttered out of the corner of my mouth, patting her hand. Chest swelling with purpose, I met the stares of my crew head on. "Vlad thinks we wanted him to be our sword. Let's show him we can change the world with a platform and a megaphone."

TEN

VLAD

I woke in a pile of leaves, shirtless and painted with blood. The soles of my feet were filthy and covered in scratches, my ribcage sliced with five distinct claw marks. Sucking air through my teeth, I pulled myself up to my knees. Pulse pounding unforgiving spikes of pain into my temples, I paused with one hand in the dirt and waited for the forest to stop spinning around me. Sticky wetness squished between my fingers. With a knot of dread tightening in my throat, I cast a hesitant stare down. Beside my thigh, an unseeing eye peered up at me from the decapitated head of a black bear. Emitting a shocked yelp, I crab crawled away from it only to slam into what remained of the furry lump of its body. Forcing myself up on shaky legs, I struggled to find north, then hobbled in that direction quick as I could. A short while later, I broke through a thatch of foliage at the edge of the forest, breathless and holding my cramping side.

There stood Dorian with a clean change of clothes thrown over his arm, and a bucket of clean water at his feet. Stumbling to his side, I fell to my knees to slurp water from the bucket by the handful.

"I killed a grizzly bear," I gasped, in between gulps.

"I'm very well aware," Dorian stated, picking dandelion fuzz off the jacket he brought. "I've been baiting the woods for them. The Dragon seems amused by the challenge of killing them, for now at least."

Splashing water over my face, I washed away a bit of the grime and gore. "I wouldn't know. The days of it taunting me with my kills seem to be behind me. For which, I'm grateful."

"Maybe it feels there's nothing worth showing ... yet. With that in mind, I have to ask—once more—are you sure you want to go through with this?" His head jerked in the direction of the suit he held.

Dipping my hands into the water, I rubbed my palms together. "Why would I change my mind?"

"Why?" Dorian parroted, eyebrows lifting in question. "How about because your blackouts are becoming more and more frequent? Or, that you *lose time* quite regularly? If you find neither of those reasons to be adequate, we could go with the ugly truth that it's not a question of *if* you're going to hurt her, but *when*."

"That's not going to happen." Rising to my feet, I reached for my shirt. "With your help, we can keep her safe. I know we can."

"What if I'm tired of helping?" Dorian freed the shirt from under its accompanying jacket, and slapped it into my hand. "I should be researching spells to rid you of The Dragon, not concocting new ways to make your life more tolerable with it."

Shrugging on the garment, I thumbed the buttons closed. "No one is stopping you from finding a spell. Please, by all means, do! In the meantime, I'm going to try with all of my might to claim somewhat of a normal life."

Sighing his annoyance, Dorian dragged one hand over the stubble on his chin. "You realize there is another bend in this particular path that we've failed to consider ..."

Bristling, I froze. "Don't say it."

Dorian's shoulders sank. "Someone has to. You need to hear it, Vlad. The Dragon used to tell you all the time that by the sacrament of blood you would solidify your bond to it and be granted control. I have had no luck finding an extraction spell that works. That may be your only option left."

Snatching my coat from his grip, I yanked it up my arms. "We will speak of this no further."

"Yes, of course. Because you have everything under control." Dorian glanced back toward town, and my Transylvanian home, feigning a yawn. "Tell me, with all that you've been gifted, how can you settle for this mediocre existence?"

Untying my hair, I combed my fingers through it, then reknotted it at the nape of my neck. "Don't confuse comfort with mediocrity."

"Horses of the same color," Dorian let one shoulder rise and fall in a dismissive shrug. "Think of all you're capable of, and what you could achieve if you were bold enough to claim it. This life is beneath you, Vlad."

I felt The Dragon role in my gut, stretching its essence in response to my hammering heart. "That's enough," I hissed through my teeth.

Eyes narrowed with interest, Dorian didn't miss a moment of my tense reaction. "It's not just this town, you know. *Jusztina* is beneath you."

The Dragon emerged with a deafening roar. Seizing Dorian by his shirt collar, I slammed his shoulder blades into the trunk of a towering oak. "You will *not* speak ill of her! Not ye who put this vile *thing* inside of me. I have spilled buckets of blood because of *you!*" *Drákon's* satanic hiss echoed through my mind, urging me to crush Dorian's windpipe beneath my forearm. Battling against that violent yearning, I fought to loosen my hold.

Eyes watering, Dorian rasped, "There it is. There's the beast you claim you can control. Can you feel it clawing to the surface? Your power over it slipping from your grasp? Does it feel good to unleash it? To let every fiber of your being feed into that hypnotic rage?"

s much as I hated to admit it, he was right. I wanted nothing more than to rip his head from his shoulders, and paint the earth with his blood. Staring hard at my white-knuckled grip of his shirt, I willed my fingers to loosen.

"You're wrong about me," I rumbled to *Drákon* as much as Dorian. "That isn't who I am."

Free from my grasp, Dorian gasped for breath with his hands on his knees. "Not yet, but it will be. Eventually, you'll give in, and lose yourself entirely. I would wager that the harder you fight, the bloodier that day will be. That's why I'm leaving. I will see you through today. After that, I can't bear to witness what is sure to follow. If I find an unbinding spell powerful enough to work, I will return. Until then, you're on your own, brother."

IN A MEADOW bursting with wildflowers, Jusztina waited. Cascades of ebony hair fell to her waist in a curtain. Plump cherry lips parted in eager anticipation. Her features, delicate as that of an angel, brightened at the sight of me. Her beauty stole the breath from my lungs, reminding me that no matter what sins lay in my past heaven sought fit to bless me with her love.

We clasped hands alongside the bubbling spring at the edge of Draculesti grounds, where rippling water lapped gently over time polished rocks and pebbles. Birds chirped a merry chorus, sunlight filtering down through the canopy of branches overhead. Jusztina's hand maiden, Elena, and Dorian acted as witnesses, standing on opposite sides of the priest who performed my baptism when I was a child, Father Van Helsing.

"Do you, Jusztina Szilágyi, take Vlad Tepes of House Draculesti to be your husband, in good times and bad, in sickness and health, to love and to honor the remainder of your days until parted by death?"

"I do," she eagerly responded.

Those two simple words ignited a blaze of glorious victory in my heart.

Unable to hold back, I caught my bride by the waist and claimed her lips with mine.

"You may now kiss the bride," Van Helsing chuckled, closing his bible with a thump.

Jusztina buried her head in the crook of my neck, giggling as I lifted her from the ground to spin us both in a joyful circle. The white fabric of her gauze gown belled out, snapping and cracking in the breeze.

One lone cloud blew in, casting ominous shadows over Dorian's features. "Til death do they part ... indeed."

ELEVEN

VINX

I sensed the sinister presence before it dared show its face. It twined in, like a satin ribbon of darkness that knotted around my throat. Inky shadows swelled around me, licking over my curves and nipping at the tender flesh of my neck. Simultaneously, I feared and longed for it.

While I gasped for air, a lover's voice murmured against my ear. "May my mind and will become one with hers. When I walk, she will walk with me. When I speak, she will echo each syllable. When I feel sorrow or lust, her heart will respond in kind. I thank you, my dark lords, for helping me. May you make the cord between myself and Vincenza strong like the chains ... of a prisoner."

I wanted to run.

To fight against his magnetic pull.

Neither of which was possible when the sweet nectar of his blood washed over my lips. He tasted like a hard rain after an arid drought.

The first flower of spring that persevered after a harsh, unforgiving winter. The lilt of a child's laugh riding a gentle breeze.

Life. Love. Happiness. Strength.

All intermingling in the heady brew he gifted me.

With each pull of his blood, invisible tendrils coiled around me, chaining me where I stood. Arms yanked out wide, legs stretched to their breaking point. I could feel his will snaking through my veins, binding my free will. I was nothing more than his puppet. A hapless marionette for him to toy with to his violent delight.

Jolting upright, I woke with a start. Sleep hadn't been my intention. Unfortunately, extreme jetlag demanded otherwise. Laying on top of the covers, the notebook I scribbled press conference ideas in slid off my leg. True to her word, Mics hadn't left my side. Slumped in an armchair in the corner, her chin drooped to her chest. Her thick rope braids fell forward, blanketing Batdog in his spot sprawled across her lap. Snoring his contentment, he filled the air with the potent smell of dog farts.

Swinging my legs over the side of the bed, I grabbed my oversized hoodie from the bench at the foot of the four-post bed and tugged it over my t-shirt. Tucking my grandmother's silver nail file into the elastic band of my cotton pajama pants, I padded to the door on bare feet. The door creaked open, its resistant hinges begging me to reconsider. What I was looking for in that twilight hour, I couldn't say. Like so many other moments of uncertainty in my life, I was pretty sure I could find whatever it was in the kitchen. My hunger awoke right along with me, causing my fangs to ache for the coppery tang of raw meat. Moving on whispered steps, I meandered the halls in search of a fridge to raid.

Flickering light from a darkened room lassoed my attention. Momentarily putting my quest for sustenance on hold, I tiptoed closer. Peeking around the corner, I found a den furnished with a blend of antiques and modern-day comforts. The far wall was a bank of television screens, all of which broadcasted news of the brewing vampire war on every station imaginable. A male figure sat perched on the edge of a ruby red loveseat, silhouetted by the glow of the screens. Forearms on his knees, he watched the slew of tragedy unfold without blinking. On the cushion beside him, a tablet showcased continuous coverage from yet another media source. Countless reports. So many points of view. Yet, the message being uttered rang with a ceaseless loop of similarity.

"If it wasn't for the humanitarian efforts of DG Enterprises ..."

"Another life saved by DG Enterprises ..."

"... A new medical advancement by DG Enterprises."

"An act of mercy from DG Enterprises ..."

"... brought to you by DG Enterprises."

The company logo, a silver DG encircled with a twining vine, flashed on three of the screens. Something about it scratched at a memory I couldn't quite recall.

A roar ripping from his throat, the shadowy figure sprang to his feet and hurled the tablet at the wall. It cracked the plaster on contact, exploding in a spray of broken plastic and circuitry. Sensing my presence, he spun in a blur, the sharp angles of his features more beast than man.

"Lord Draculesti?" I managed, feeling I stumbled into a rattle snake pit.

Physically shaking off the effects of his outburst, he bowed his head in a chivalrous show of respect. "A thousand apologies, Miss Larow. I believed myself to be alone. Elsewise, I would never have behaved in such a fashion."

"No apology needed." Clearing my throat, I hunted for some passable variation of my normal voice. "If I had a nickel for every tablet I dropped or smashed I would have ..." that's the moment I realized the awkward flaw in my story, "ten cents. It's only happened twice."

And that, kids, is how you make yourself look like a complete asshole in front of the King of Night.

Glancing over his shoulder, he peered at the remains of the shattered tablet. "It's an infuriating device. If it's going to spew such ugliness, it should be notably more durable."

"I don't think they're meant to be spiked by a vampire god." Crossing one ankle over the other, I leaned against the door frame and jerked my chin toward the screens. "Although, I am encouraged by you being riled up over the circumstances. Makes me hopeful you'll reconsider joining our cause."

Without a word, he strode to the window, peering out at the amethyst sky that marked the setting sun.

I shoved off the wall, risking a step closer. "You saw through my eyes, along with the footage. Your own son is buried in this so deep, there's no way he can claw his way out alone. He's devoted his life to honoring your teachings by helping others. Now, he's the one that needs help. We can still save him, if you join us."

Tendons of his jaw tightening, Vlad bitterly shook his head. "Rau was a sweet child that lost his loving mother far too soon. I never wanted this life for him. I sought to protect him, and keep him unmarred by this damning curse. Still, he is and always will be my son. I would save him now … if I could."

Wincing, I rapidly blinked in confusion. "Dude, you're the first of the Nosferatu kind, and inspiration for countless monster movies! The mere mention of your name evokes fear in the hearts of your enemies. We're up against posturing politicians. You drop fang *once* in front of them and they'll soil their tighty-whities *and* make a public apology to all vampire-kind."

Heels sinking into the thick nap of the taupe rug, Vlad glanced my way over his shoulder. "How can you fight, when you don't even know your true enemy?"

Lacing my fingers together, I dropped my hands in front of me to squash my growing desire to throttle Dracula. Which, even in my jetlagged state, seemed like a monumentally bad idea. "The enemy seems pretty straight forward. They are a bunch of narrow-minded bigots who would rather take innocent lives than to let go of their preconceived notions of our kind."

Vlad's stare drifted once more to the continuous news coverage. "Those people are nothing more than pawns, easily moved and maneuvered by their own hatred. The real enemy is one far more dangerous."

"*Markus*," lip curling in disgust, I jabbed my hand in the direction of the screen playing his latest bullshit interview, "has *literally* killed to further the segregation of the Nosferatu people. He thrives off of hatred. The idea of being up against someone worse than *him* is chilling."

"You should be more than chilled. You should be paralyzed with fear to the very marrow of your bones." Closing the gap of space between us, Vlad rose to full height and peered down the bridge of his nose at me. Shadows darkened the shallows of his cheeks, blacking out his eyes in a trick of light that made him appear every bit the demi-god of death. "For, how can you fight someone who craves nothing but the bloody chaos of war? He feels nothing. Wants for nothing. Longs only to tear everything, and everyone apart. His great victory would be watching the world burn. My advice, *copil*? Grab those you love, and run. Hide in the farthest reaches of the earth, and pray he never finds you."

Dragging my fingers through my hair, I trudged my way through his ominous warning to the heart of truth buried beneath. "I don't know what history you have with this mysterious terror, but people I care about are caught up in this. One way or another, I have to get them out."

I'm sure in some book of etiquette it was considered rude for me to turn my back on a man of his station. For the life of me, I couldn't begin to care. I came in search of hope, not cowardice. Offering no explanation, I shook my head and strode for the door.

"What will you do?" Vlad's head tilted, his gaze sharpening with something that resembled respect.

"Now?" One hand on the doorframe, I glanced back with a bitter attempt at a smile. "Right now, I'm going to get something to eat. Then, I'll unleash holy hell if that's what it takes."

"Miss Larow?" The Son of the Dragon called after me, his tone an alluring pool of lapping warmth. "Would you honor me with a hunt?"

Stopping short, my eyes bulged. Hunting with Dracula. That was like the marijuana enthusiast's equivalent of toking up with Willie Nelson.

He clasped his hands behind his back, dipping his chin in a brief nod of encouragement. "Blood is life … and strength. It is wise for you to feed for the fight to come."

TWELVE

VINX

We moved between the trees with feline fluidity, springing over saplings and repelling off boulders. Barefoot, the night air caught the loose fabric of our clothing, snapping it behind us like cresting waves. Following Vlad's trail, I couldn't help but marvel at his beauty. Before, I viewed him as an untouchable myth, a monument among men. His striking truth revealed itself in ghostly quiet strides through the moonlit forest. Shirt blowing open, the muscles of his sculpted torso worked with the synchronized poetry of a galloping stallion. A current of hair, the hue of polished sandstone, danced around his face. Tipping his chin skyward he sniffed the air, a scruff of whiskers accentuating the sharp cut of his jawline. Ethereal green eyes pierced the foliage, searching for traces of movement.

There, riding the pine scented breeze, came a whiff of possibility. Head whipping in Vlad's direction, I watched hunger dilate his pupils to tarry black pits. Jerking his forehead toward Polaris—the North Star—he pointed me in the direction of the alluring smell.

While Vlad dashed around the perimeter to box in our prey, I ducked under a low-hanging branch and fell into a crouch. There she was, a stunning doe lapping water from the brook. Thirst curled my lip from my teeth, allowing my fangs to lengthen.

Before I could venture a step, Vlad slunk into the clearing. He made no attempts to hide himself, but cautiously approached the skittish creature with one-hand raised before him. Clucking his tongue against the roof of his mouth, he drew her attention to him. Survival instincts should have screamed for her to bolt.

Not this night.

Not with *him*.

Contradicting nature's laws, the timid beauty risked a step toward him, then another. Holding perfectly still, he quietly shushed her as she neared. A silvery beam of moonlight danced between the canopy of leaves overhead, illuminating his predatory splendor. His fangs remained tucked away, his motions deliberate and thoughtful.

Dipping his head, he met her transfixed stare. To my absolute astonishment, the russet doe ... offered him her throat.

"No fucking way," I murmured.

Vlad motioned me over with the twitch of two upturned fingers. "Come, slow and easy."

Toes sinking into the dew-covered grass, I inched my way over to kneel beside them.

Laying a hand to the doe's neck, Vlad stroked her coarse coat. "Her loving gift should never be repaid by the pain of our vile affliction."

"Y-you want me to lick her to numb it?" I stammered, feeling every bit the awkward baby vamp.

Vlad hitched one brow, amusement tugging at the corners of his mouth. "You can feed from her, but deem a lick foul?"

"I know, I sound like one of those selfish asshats that scoff at their roll in a sixty-nine." Closing my eyes for a beat, I said a silent prayer of thanks that I was no longer able to blush. "You can ask your Court to explain what that is later."

"I know what a *şaizeci şi nouă* is, *copil*. The young didn't invent the pleasures of the flesh. They just came up with new names for them." Shifting his weight onto the balls of his feet, he supported the doe's head with his palm. "To be clear, there is no need to lick her. I used my influence to dull any pain she would have felt. You need only feed, while she's calm in her offering."

My vision zeroed in on the thick vein in her neck throbbing with life. Head turned, I lunged for that addictive pulse. She gave little more than a shudder as my incisors pierced her hide. One heady pull, and warmth flooded my lips in an intoxicating current. Falling back on my rump, I pulled her on to my lap, cradled protectively in my hold.

"That's enough." Vlad laid a gentle hand to my arm.

Nose wrinkled into a snarl, I snapped in his direction, an inhuman growl rumbling through my teeth.

Eyes flashing with a deadly gleam, Vlad dropped fang. "*Stop, or you'll kill her.*"

Something deep within me recognized him as the alpha and slapped me from the fog of bloodlust. Hands on either side of the doe's chest, I patiently guided her up on wobbly legs. "Should I heal her?"

Brow furrowed, Vlad peered at the blood streaking from her puncture wounds. "I don't know enough about the properties of your blood to trust it."

He ground the tip of his index finger into the point of his fang, then applied pressure until one ruby droplet swelled from his flesh. Rubbing that restorative elixir over her wounds closed them in an instant. Offering a snort of thanks, the doe flipped her head toward the bank of trees and bounded off into the night.

"You speak of our kind with disgust, but that was nothing short of beautiful," I gasped with audible awe.

Rising to his feet, Vlad watched the dear's white-cotton puff tail disappear from sight. "Don't ever confuse what we are with loveliness of any sort. One way or another, death *always* claims those foolish enough to be near us."

With those as his parting words, he stalked in the direction of the castle without a glance back. Only then did I realize he hadn't fed.

THIRTEEN

VLAD

"Stay with me, my love." It would have taken a stronger man than I to refuse my beloved's request. Staring up at me with emerald eyes, she batted her lashes and tempted me with a coy pout. "The baby and I miss you when you're away." To further her point, she rubbed a hand over her swollen midsection, ripe with child.

Seated on the settee at the foot of our bed, I cast my stare toward the window. Slashes of orange and pink zigzagged across the sky, the late day sun sinking in the horizon. As of late, night brought on more of my episodes, forcing me to take drastic measures.

Tucking one leg beneath me, I turned to face my beautiful bride. Lounging on our bed, her back was propped up by a mountain of pillows. "The dungeon is safer, *floare*. I can shackle myself in the farthest cell and not have to worry about harming anyone."

One hand supporting the weight of her belly, Jusztina scooched my way on her knees. Her nightgown slid up, teasing me with the curve of her alabaster thighs. "I know you fear that thing that roosts within you. Even so, I shan't believe for even an instant that you would *ever* harm me." Noticing how my chin drooped to my chest, she shifted to a new tactic. "Plus, I've felt stirrings from the little one today. I would hate for her—"

"Him," I corrected with a soft smile.

Lacing her fingers behind my neck, she pressed her forehead to mine. "He *or* she, would prefer you be here when they come into the world. Oh please, Vlad?" She pleaded, peppering my face with kisses. "Hold me while I sleep? I need to feel you beside me."

As I rubbed my fingers over her forearm, I caught sight of my wrist, chaffed an angry red from the shackles I clasped on each night. "How about this?" I bargained, kissing the tip of her nose. "I'll stay until you fall asleep, then I'll venture to the bowels of the castle for my own piece of mind."

"If our time together is limited, we mustn't waste a moment." Settling back against the pillows, Jusztina wriggled under the blankets and beckoned me to join her with the curl of one finger. "The baby is restless. If we're still you may be able to feel the kicks."

I molded my body to hers and snuggled in. Reaching over her belly, I let her guide my hand to the proper place. If the baby squirmed, I didn't feel it. My attentions were fixated on the setting sun, and what I feared would follow.

By the time the sky deepened from brilliant violet to deep sapphire Jusztina was sound asleep. Curled in my arms, her sweet serenity revealed itself in a contented snore.

I was attempting to wiggle my arm out from under her when I felt the first twitch. Moving by a will not my own, my traitorous fingers curled into a claw on Jusztina's belly. Throwing a confining leg over hers, I pinned her to the mattress, breath coming in ragged pants. Darkness didn't creep into the edges of my vision. Nor did I fade into a cloud of black. I felt every inkling of The Dragon's pleasures rolling through me in malicious waves. He meant to paint the walls with my wife's blood ... while I watched.

I planted a hand on the mattress, channeling every bit of my weakening resolve, and shoved myself off the bed.

Stirring in the chill of my absence, Jusztina rolled onto her elbow. "Vlad? Darling, are you okay?"

"*Get out*," I hissed, palms slapping the floor in my frantic crawl away from her. "Run ... *now!*"

Face draining ashen, she pulled herself up on to her knees. "Is it The Dragon? Can you get to the dungeon?"

"There isn't time," I forced the words through my teeth, the blood scorching through my veins. "I ... can't hold it back ... long. Please, *dragoste, go and call for the guard!*" My fingernails dug into floor, clawing divots in the wood planks.

I both loved and hated her for hesitating. Face crumbling, tears slipped from her lashes. Both hands protectively cradling her belly, she backed off the bed. "I'm sorry. I'm so sorry," she sniveled. She filled her lungs, braced herself, then bolted for the door. Skirting around me, she escaped down the hall.

Or, did she?

By the glow of the candles lighting our bed chamber, I could see my reflection perfectly in the window opposite me. In that mirrored universe, I lunged for Jusztina the instant she ventured within arm's reach. Catching her by the hair, I yanked her back and held her to my chest with one merciless hand to her throat. Tears flowing down her face in torrents, she shielded her belly with her arms. While I couldn't hear her cries, I knew she was pleading with this monstrous version of me to think of our child. The vision was so real, so utterly horrifying, I glanced down at my own hands expecting to find the treacherous limbs actually choking the life from my terrified bride. One blink, and blood covered them in a thick slick of gore. A second, and they were clean. Stumbling forward, I squinted at the mysterious alternate reality playing out within the glass.

"Is this what you think it will look like when your greatest fears are realized?" A familiar voice bounced off the stone walls, echoing all around. "When the normal life you've fought so hard for is destroyed by your hand?"

"Dorian?" I called, turning in a slow circle in search of him.

His form stretched from the shadows, birthed from absolute darkness. "I feared you wouldn't recognize me, brother." While the being before me wore the face of my friend, my skin prickled with icy awareness that he was *not* the same man who rode from Transylvania two years prior. His regal clothing looked handmade from the finest fabrics. The once unruly mop of his hair had been tamed into a sleek swoop across his forehead. Gold-jeweled rings decorated his fingers, which were steepled beneath his chin. A bout of good fortune could have led to those alterations. It was what I saw in his eyes that warned of a pivotal change. Where once a light of kindness brightened his ocean blue stare, now remained a vast sea of ... nothingness.

"How did you get here? Are ye taking pleasure in watching my wife sleep?"

Prowling through the room, Dorian's shoulders shook with a chuckle. "My tastes have matured far beyond simple voyeurism. Not that I didn't once enjoy overhearing her mews of ecstasy during my stay here. She is a vocal little thing, isn't she?"

"Do not speak such filth about my wife!" I bellowed, hands curling into fists at my sides.

Turning on his heel to face me, Dorian's head cocked with interest. "Or, what? You'll call forth The Dragon? Tell me, did its stirrings still once I appeared?" Not giving me a chance to confirm such a claim, he tapped the point of his chin with his index finger. "Hmmm ... what do you suppose that means?"

I thought to argue otherwise, to declare I was moments from tearing his head from his shoulders. However, the truth held my tongue. He was right. *Drákon* fell dormant, quiet as a sleeping babe. "You've learned to influence The Dragon. I assume that means you've finally come to claim it?"

Rolling his eyes, Dorian's posture sagged with annoyance. "I no longer wish to be infected by that *parasite*."

"Since we were boys, that's all you ever wanted. What great revelation would prompt you to give up that quest?"

Fiddling with his pinkie ring, Dorian paced the length of my chamber. "When I left here, it was out of fear of what was inside you. I sought strength by any magical means necessary to battle what I feared was yet to come."

"I've never blamed you, Dorian. We were children. You did what you felt you must to—"

"Oh, don't misunderstand. I'm not plagued with guilt over the matter," traces of laughter bubbled through his tone. "Quite the opposite, in fact. I'm *giddy* with anticipation at how this whole saga will unfold. As I was saying, I went in search of power, and found far more than I could ever imagine. It began with an ancient script describing a truly remarkable spell. One that required the rendering of a portrait. I sat days for it. It had to be perfect, you see, to capture the very essence of me. Once complete, I uttered the words that would bind me to that canvas for all eternity."

"W-what are you saying?" I stammered, failing to follow what seemed a questionable recollection.

Plucking a bit of fuzz from his navy coat, Dorian rolled it between his thumb and forefinger and flicked it to the ground. "I'm saying, I mastered immortality. I can move through this world untouched by age, sin, or harm. The portrait absorbs all of that bothersome mess, granting me invincibility."

"That's ludicrous. Such a thing is impossible." Even as I uttered the words, I caught glimpses of the certainty behind them. The visible void within Dorian, that emotional disconnect from the spark of life, both hinted that his tie to humanity had been severed. If that was true, whatever made Dorian who he was—as the friend I loved and trusted—must have been trapped within the canvas of that portrait.

"Says the man possessed by a demon." Grabbing Jusztina's hair brush from her bedside table, Dorian flipped it over in his hand and extracted one lone strand from between its bristles.

Fearing his intent, a strode over to swat both brush and hair from his hands. "Enough of these games and diversions. *Why are you here?*"

Features blank of emotion, Dorian swept his arm in front of him in a dramatic arc. At the motion, an invisible force lassoed me by the middle. Thrown against the wall hard enough to knock the air from my lungs, his power pinned me there.

The heels of his shoes clicking over the floor boards, Dorian calmly sauntered to my side. "What's this?" he gasped in mock confusion. "The famed warrior—whose name evokes fear in the hearts of his enemies—rendered defenseless? Isn't this normally the moment where *Drákon* appears in an explosion of violence and mayhem? Perhaps you should call out to him? Go ahead. Give it a try. It'll be funny."

"Why are you doing this?" I grunted, struggling against his hold.

Planting one hand on the wall beside me, Dorian leaned in close enough for his hair to tickle my cheek. "Because, it's time for you to submit ... to what's inside you."

Pulling my head back as far as I could manage, I glared daggers of hate his way. "And damn my soul for all eternity? You've gone mad!"

Head tilted, he considered that option. "No, not mad. *Bored.* You see, after becoming immortal I embarked on a rigorous experimentation process to determine if it was, indeed, true. Small at first. A cut to the hand. A sip of diluted poison. When I immediately healed, or suffered no ill-effects, I moved on to more ... interesting stakes. No matter what I tried, the hand of death couldn't touch me. Even so, I feared the wrath of God. Surely, such an all-powerful being could strike me down if He saw fit? That, my friend, is where the real fun started. I tested the All-Mighty with some truly deplorable acts. I mean, really *vile* deeds that would make Lucifer blush." Pushing off the wall, he took a step back and spun in a slow circle. "Yet here I stand, unmarred by His wrath. The tragic part of all of this? With the urgency of a limited lifespan removed, it's become far harder for me to claim a ... *thrill* of any sort."

"*That's* why you want me to submit to The Dragon?" I spat. "That you may have *companionship* as you wander the earth until Judgement Day?"

"You took *that* from what I said?" Dorian's mouth screwed to the side. "I feel part of my message got lost in translation. Simply put, there's a demon inside of you, and I can't be killed! I want to lure it all the way out, maybe poke it with a stick to get it good and riled up, then see what that unholy monster can do!"

Head falling back against the wall with a thump, I shook my head. "You would damn my soul for your own entertainment?"

A beat of silence as he blinked my way. "Yes. I thought I made that quite clear."

"You heartless bastard." Thrusting one shoulder forward, then the other, I fought for freedom. "This has all been for naught. I have withstood *Drákon's* thrall this long. I won't give in to indulge your *sick* fascination."

Jabbing one hand on his hip, Dorian wagged his index finger in my direction. "It wouldn't be fun if it was as simple as *your prerogative.* I've lined up fascinating methods meant solely to motivate your decision. The first of which will be arriving in just a few days' time. You see, my travels led me back to Ruler Murad's plentiful domain. He was eager to hear the stories I regaled of your new life outside of his service. Unfortunately for you, I *did* take creative liberties with tales of your diminished loyalty. As far as he knows, you've been rallying soldiers in preparation of an uprising against the Ottoman Empire."

Dorian chose that moment to release his mystical hold, sending me stumbling for footing. "What have you done?"

"You're wise to be concerned." His head bobbed in encouragement. "Murad did *not* take lightly to this news. Especially knowing you possess intricate details about his armies. The fact that you have the coordinates to each of the base camps is enough to lead to their downfall. That caused Murad to take incredibly drastic measures ..."

Dorian trailed off, waiting for me to take the bait and ask the question he was twitching to answer. "What measures?"

eyes widening with manic glee, Dorian sat on the foot of my bed and crossed his legs at the ankles. "He *immediately* formed an alliance with the Saxons in exchange for possession of your lands once you're defeated."

A haze of black wrath stained the corners of my vision. For the first time, it had nothing whatsoever to do with my dark passenger. "You've cursed my family, and all the residents here to death." Each word scorched on my tongue like a branding iron. "I could kill you, you treacherous wretch."

"Actually," he pointed out, launching off the mattress, "you can't. That's the point of this whole rigamarole. You should also know that until you commit yourself to The Dragon, I will be able to manipulate it to my will. Yet another dark magic trick I picked up. That said, were you to submit, you could unleash its full fury, *and* protect Transylvania. Just a little something to think about."

Nostrils flaring, I stalked a circle around him. "And if I don't?"

Crossing one arm over his middle, Dorian rested the opposite elbow on it to support his chin in his palm. "If you don't, Murad and his soldiers will storm this village and slice the life out of you. In which case The Dragon will be forced to find another vessel, and I can continue my pursuit."

"The dunes at the edge of the valley offer a great vantage point of the entire village." My chest rose and fell in fevered pants.

"How thoughtful, you don't want me to miss a moment of the spectacle!" Dorian mused with a playful clap of his hands.

"No." For the first time, I found myself missing *Drákon's* writhing from within. "Because I want you to stay and watch. Once this is over it won't matter where you hide. I will find you, and I *will* kill you.

FOURTEEN

VINX

Still buzzing from my hunt, I skid around the corner into my room, hoping to shower off the grime before the house roused for the night. Easing the door shut, I flicked on the light, and spun to find a figure lounging on my bed.

"Have you heard the latest?" Hands behind his head, Carter's long legs were crossed at the ankle.

I handled the surprise in cool, vampress fashion. Meaning I squealed, threw myself backwards, and banged my funny bone on the doorknob.

"Nice *creature of the night* reflexes." Carter mused with the lift of one eyebrow.

"You're lucky I don't lead with the fang!" Granted, my heart couldn't race, but it *did* give one harried lurch in objection. "What in Vlad's name are you doing sneaking into my room?"

Kicking his legs over the side of the bed, he pushed to sitting and dropped his hands in his lap. "Vamp hours combined with jetlag aren't working for me. I couldn't sleep, so I turned on the news. What I saw ..." trailing off, he chewed on his lower lip. "It was bad. I came in here to talk to you about it. When you weren't here, I figured you found somewhere to follow the broadcasts and were glued to a screen. Now that I see your crusted blood mustache, I'm thinking I was way off the mark there."

"Couldn't find anything in the kitchen," I lied, wiping my mouth on the back of my hand.

"So ... you settled for one of the townsfolk?"

Shoulders sagging, I glared up at him from under my lashes. "Hardly. Venison was on the menu. But, I *do* need a shower. Maybe we can pause this convo until I—"

That's as far as I made it before the door burst open, spilling Elodie and Thomas into the room.

"Did you tell her?" Stern expression firmly in place, Elodie acknowledged Carter with a lift of her chin.

"I was about to. Got momentarily distracted by her looking like an extra from a zombie movie." Carter jabbed his thumb in my direction.

Thomas sniffed the air, his nose crinkling. "You smell like moss and deer piss."

Jabbing my hands on my hips, I rolled my eyes. "As much as I enjoy all of you bursting in to insult my personal hygiene, how about if you get to the point of why you're here?"

"That vampire refugee camp we took you to?" Elodie waited for me to nod before continuing. "Somehow, Markus and his people found a way to dose every vamp there with artificial sulfur. *All* of them are on a spree through New Haven, looting and tearing the city apart. The town lines have been blockaded under a state of emergency. The military has been sent in armed with silver-laced ammunition."

Leaning one elbow on top of the antique bureau, Thomas rubbed his hand over the back of his neck. "Our plans to go back are destroyed. Not only could we not land a plane there if we wanted to, but the public persona you've built isn't broad enough to stand against something of this magnitude, Vinx. You're known primarily in Connecticut. We need someone with a more global pull."

Elodie planted herself at the foot of the bed, and crossed her arms over her middle. "We need *Rau*."

"Or, *Vlad*," Carter added.

Slumping against the wall, I melted to the floor. "That won't work. Not now. Even mentioning Vlad's awake will fuel the panic. The media will spin it that it was the buckets of blood being spilled that woke him."

"*You!*" A deathly rattle rasped from the open doorway. Hood pulled back, a formerly cloaked member of the Court drifted into the mix. To my astonishment, his appearance was far more haunting *without* that woolen shield. Leathered skin stretched taut over bone. Sunken features were stained a deep, bruise purple. Flanked by an indifferent Rage, he rolled one gnarled hand from beneath his draped sleeve to stab a knotty finger in my direction. "I saw you with him, out in the woods."

Pushing off the bureau, Thomas snapped to attention. "Brother Renfield, you've broken your vow of silence!"

Wincing as if each word pained him, the skeletal being I now knew as Renfield smacked cracked and arid lips. "She and the master hunted together, and … *he gave her his prey.*"

A chorus of shocked gasps fluttered through the room. Even Carter blinked my way in astonished disbelief.

"I knew I heard voices!" Micah stepped from the bathroom dressed in a robe. Squeezing water from her hair with a terry cloth towel, she recoiled the instant she caught a whiff. "Ugh, why does it smell like a petting zoo in here?"

"That smell," Elodie gulped, "would be Vincenza. It seems she … *hunted with Vlad.*"

Batdog wove between Micah's feet, scampering to my side to paint my face with sloppy kisses.

Groaning at Elodie's melodramatic announcement, I scratched the rump of my wriggly little furball. "Everyone keep their pants on, geez. It was *one* hunt. You all need to simmer down."

Hands falling limp to her sides, the towel slipped from Micah's fingers and floated to a heap on the floor. "Vinx, have you forgotten *everything* I taught you? All of our lessons on vampire traditions and practices?"

"No!" I countered with an indignant flare. "I put a pin in *anything* that could prevent me from getting killed. Which seemed like a stellar strategy." Six sets of eyes burned into me without blinking. "Although, now I'm feeling I've missed a crucial factor in this equation. Anyone want to clue an undead sister in?"

"There is only *one* reason a male Nosferatu of his station would deliver food to a female, and allow her to feed first." Thomas bumped my hip with his heel, patiently waiting for me to catch up.

Peering up at him, I shook my head and shrugged.

Elodie sighed in annoyance. "Because ... he views her as a suitable, potential mate."

Eyebrows disappearing into my hairline, all I could manage was a shocked, "*Huh?*"

"Something about her must have struck a chord with him." Micah peered my way, like she wanted to examine me under a microscope. "How fascinating."

Slapping my palms to the wall behind me, I shimmied up to standing. "Okay, can we all agree we might be overreacting to this just a tad?"

A ripple of fabric, and Renfield stood directly in front of me. "You must marry him!"

"Or, you know, we could hurdle straight into insanity."

Catching my chin with the crook of his decrepit finger, Renfield turned my head in one direction then the other. "You're homely compared to his first wife, Jusztina. However, dim lighting may work in your favor."

"Like you're Chris Hemsworth?" I jabbed, swatting his hand away.

Catching hold of my fingers, he held them tight in both hands. "Without that nuptial bond, I fear we will lose him again. In our time, the fact that you aren't much to look at would have paled in light of doing one's duty by honoring the marital vows."

"I liked you better as a silent, scary-ass phantom."

"What happened to Jusztina shattered his heart. He never fully recovered. Since then, I have witnessed him showing *no* interest in any woman." The blood red orbs of his eyes gazed upon me with awestruck appreciation. "Until you, a scientifically engineered mutt."

Giving his hand a squeeze, I dropped my voice to a supportive whisper. "Is this your first time ever trying to compliment someone? You're not good at it."

Face a mask of concentration, Elodie pressed her index finger to her lips. "He might be on to something. We could use this. A relationship between the two of them might give us the larger platform we need. With all the brutality splashed on every news channel, we flip the narrative. We sell people on the fairytale romance between the Nosferatu god and vampress nobody. The media will be banging down the door to cover the story of the century. Then, we weave our statements into what they think are going to be cutesy fluff pieces."

Suddenly feeling insanely exposed, I curled my shoulders inward and covered myself with my arms. "By pimping me out to the King of the Undead? I'm going to go ahead and take a hard pass."

"Seriously?" Micah *tsk*ed. "You don't think he's hot in a kingly, *call me Daddy*, kind of way?"

"First of all," I cringed, stabbing a finger of judgment in her direction. "Not that. *Never* that. We as a collective society need to agree that *daddy* shit is gross and icky. Secondly, yes. I'm very serious about not being prostituted."

Absentmindedly, Thomas scratched at the stump of his severed hand. "It's not prostitution. It's politics."

Shoving himself off the squeaky mattress, Carter's face folded with regret. "More to the point, Vinx, it may be our only option."

"This is insane!" I exclaimed, casting a glare of blame on each of them. "Let's circle back to the 'Why is Vlad Awake' argument, shall we? A staged romance isn't going to prevent whispers that he snapped to just in time for a vampire uprising!"

At that, they fell silent.

"Oh, for Vlad's sake!" Rage broke the hush with an exasperated groan from her post by the door. "The level of stupid in this room physically pains me. Has *no one* read or watched any of that teeny-bopper vampire-romance drivel? This is *standard* love story crap. It has been a ritual of the Court for, like, ever to bleed over the seal at Vlad's tomb on every full moon. So, say her service to the Nosferatu community earned her a place on the Court. She moved in, and joined in her first bloodsharing. Vlad got a taste, saw into her soul—or some bullshit like that—and had to wake and make her his. Really, it's pretty simple. But, if you all need me to draw you a diagram with stick figures, I can."

Defeat stealing over his features, Carter's head tilted. Locks of golden hair fell across his forehead in a charming disarray. "It's the right thing to do, Vinx. Even if I do hate it to the depths of my soul."

Dragging my hands through my hair, I tried to find *any* other alternative we failed to consider. "And, you're all *okay* with me manipulating the *Prince of Darkness* into a relationship? No one sees that as a problematic scenario?"

Renfield sauntered in a slow circle around me, dragging his stare up and down my length. "I will tell my Lord the truth about our agenda. Without a handsome dowry, or wide-brimmed hat to cover her harshly human features, I feel that will be the only way to sway him in our favor."

"I'm just going to say it, man, you're kind of a dick." I stated, chin tucked to my chest.

"This is our plan, then? We're really going to do this? Create some undead fairytale?" Bringing his hands together in a sharp clap, Carter swiveled on the ball of his foot, waiting for someone to confirm the agenda.

Arms swinging slack at her sides, Rage's head fell back. "*Yes!* Do you want it chiseled in flippin' stone? The group decided that after *tedious* discussion! *Ugh!* You are all the *worst!*" With that as her parting sentiment, Rage stomped off down the hall.

"For a human she completely lacks in compassion … or civility. I'll go talk with Lord Draculesti at once. The moment I have a response, I shall return." Renfield flipped his hood up, then floated from the room like the specter he resembled.

Chest filling with a plethora of sentiments left unsaid, Carter feigned an enthusiastic grin that landed closer to a pained grimace. "Alright! Let's do this. Vinx and Vlad, sitting in a tree. I'm going to go have a drink … or three."

FIFTEEN
VINX

A soft knock rattled the door of my suite. Stretched out on the bed, hands folded over my stomach, I stared up at the tapestry canopy without moving. Gold roses vined through a sky of crimson velvet. I had laid there long enough to follow the path of each branch of intricate embroidery to the bushel of roses at its end.

"Vinx? I know you're in there. Open the door."

"It's not locked." Rolling on my side, I turned my back to the door.

Padding in quietly, Carter eased the door shut behind him with a soft click. Taking a seat at the foot of the bed, I felt the shift of the mattress beneath his weight. "I talked to Renfield. Vlad agreed to this crazy plan. A public announcement is being made later today. Interviews are *already* being scheduled. But none of that means *anything* if you don't want to do this. Just say the word, and we're gone. We'll find another way."

"You heard Renfield. This may be my only chance to land a man."

"That's not funny, or true."

Sitting up, I curled my legs under me. "No, none of this is funny." I palmed the remote, clicking on the wall-mounted television.

Screams filled the room. On the screen, vampires burst through clouds of black smoke. Crimson tears streaked their blister-pocked cheeks. Some fell to the ground, frantically clawing for escape while their flesh boiled.

"In response to the recent outbreak of Nosferatu attacks in New Haven, the national guard has been called in." The newscaster's voice over explained with calm indifference. "The footage you are seeing is of silver-laced smoke bombs being released into the heart of the frenzy. While we have no word on if there have been any human causalities, all surviving Nosferatu at the scene will be taken into custody. From there, they will be transported to facilities donated by DG Enterprises. All of which are specifically designed to contain vampires."

Tears burning behind my eyes, my voice dropped to a raspy whisper. "They can kill and maim us in plain sight, without just cause or repercussions. To them, our lives hold no value outside of their own twisted delights. We need to rally the Nosferatu people, along with *all* our supporters. By standing together, we can shout to the world that our opposers do not decide who or what we are. *We* do. If taking part in some fairytale romance farce is going to put a mic in my hand, that can reach hundreds of thousands, then that is *exactly* what I'm going to do."

His hand drifting to mine, Carter dragged his thumb over my knuckles. "Why does it have to be *you*?"

Reaching out, I smoothed his hair behind his ear, letting my fingers linger against the silken strands. "Because, *this* is what I've been training for. Since the day I woke up on Micah's table, everything has been preparing me … for *this*. At one time, I thought

I was meant to be the executioner of the vampire movement. Now, I'd like nothing more than to be its salvation."

"Where is my place in all of this?" He asked more to himself than me.

"Where do you want it to be?"

Catching hold of my hand, he clapped it over his heart, allowing me to feel the steady drum of his resolve. "By your side, until the very end."

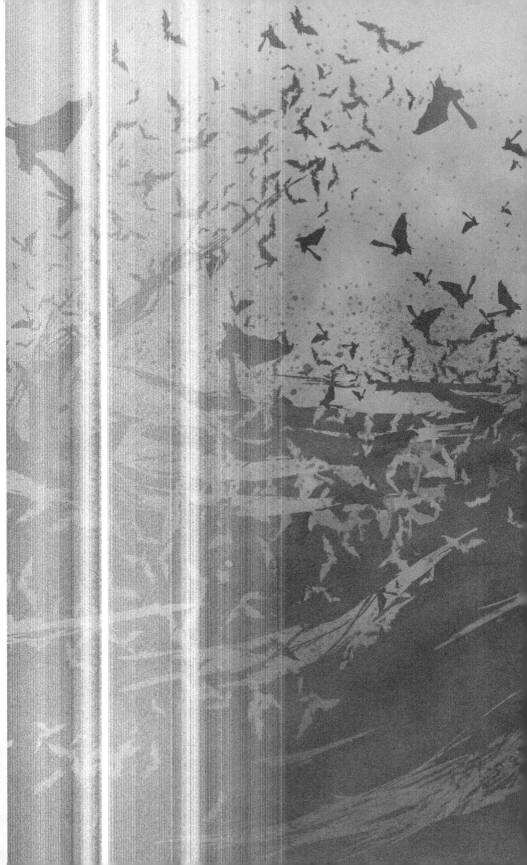

SIXTEEN
VLAD

"Jusztina!" Bolting into the kitchen, after securing all the windows in the tower rooms, I sprinted in to pull the shutters. "*Jusztina!*"

Clutching her knitting needles to her chest, as if such things could protect her, she crept from the sitting room to find me in the dining chamber. "I-is it The Dragon, Vlad? Has something happened?"

"It has, yet this time *Drákon* isn't to blame. I've called to the guards. They will be stationed atop the wall surrounding the square." Catching her by the hand, I led her toward the stairs, ignoring her hesitation with firm yet gentle insistence. "Go up to our chambers, bolt the door, and stay there. When it's safe, Renfield—you've met him, he's Commander of the Transylvanian Guard—will come for you. Open the door for *no one* else." Spinning on her, I collected both her delicate hands in mine. "Do you understand? *No one* else!"

Jusztina's chin quivered, tears tangling in her lashes. "How could I understand? You've told me nothing. What's happening, Vlad? Why must I hide?"

Afraid to lose the advantage of time, I resumed my hustle up the stairs. "Dorian convinced the Ottoman Empire that I have been plotting an uprising against them. To counter such a threat, Ruler Murad joined with the Saxons. They are headed this way, in search of answers ... or my head."

Covering her shocked gasp with porcelain fingertips, Jusztina quaked with fear. "What possible reason could he have for committing such a wicked deception?"

"Long story short? He's a horrible person." At the top of the stairs, I slammed shut the small circular window any skilled archer could easily sail an arrow through. "Once I know you're safe, I will ride out of town and set up camp. There I will stay, to intercept them when they arrive. With any luck, I can convince Murad my loyalties remain in place."

Planting her feet, Jusztina pulled against me. "If he doesn't, you'll be killed! Vlad you mustn't!"

Bed chamber in sight, I fought the urge to fling her over my shoulder and carry her the remaining distance. "What other choice have I? What would you have me do, wife?"

"My cousin, Matthias Corvinus!" She erupted, face brightening at the idea. "He's the King of Hungary! You could beseech him in my name, and seek his aid!"

"There's no time!" With an adamant shake of my head, I inched us closer to my desired destination. "Far too soon, they'll be at our gates."

Slipping her hands from my grasp, she placed her palms against my chest. "It's *you* that they want. That is a sacrifice *I'm* not ready to make, even if you are. Go, *now*. Talk to Matthias. Murad will be far more inclined to halt and listen it you are backed by the Hungarian army. Peace may yet be achieved."

Squeezing my eyes shut for a beat, I fought to suppress the blaze of hope my beloved ignited within me. Such a flame was far too dangerous to feed. "If I am not here when they arrive, they could torch the village simply to make a point. I dare not think of what they would do if they found you."

"I will borrow clothes from my handmaiden, Elena, and stay with her family while you're away. I'm perfectly capable of convincing people that I'm her cousin ..." her mouth opened, brain ticking in search of a name," ... *Mena*, visiting from my family's modest cabin in the mountains."

Cradling her face in my palms, I kissed the tip of her pert nose. "I have no doubt you could achieve a brilliant rouse. Even so, I dare not take that risk."

"You can, and you *will*." Placing her hand over mine, Jusztina returned my kiss with one planted to the heel of my palm. "Your family needs you, Vlad. Transylvania needs you. It is your duty to all those that rely on you, that you go. Travel safe, husband, knowing that I shall light candles and pray that Matthias will grant us the mercy of his favor."

SEVENTEEN

VINX

*D*racula lives.

Splashed across every media outlet, each article was accompanied by the glamourized reason for his awakening.

Namely, me.

Interview requests flooded in. The world eager to get a glimpse of the King, and future Queen of Darkness.

Nope. Nowhere near comfortable with that title.

Counting down to our first on-air appearance, it fell to Micah to transform me into a believable royal. "One upside of having Vlad's limitless wealth? We were able to hire fashion designers to create these *killer* looks."

"Killer. *Ha*. Vampire pun intended," I muttered, applying a fresh sheen of gloss to my lips.

Ignoring my stellar display of wit, Mics continued to tighten the ties of my brandy-hued bodice. Thankfully, breathing wasn't an issue. She made sure there was no room for such a novelty. "Seriously, the way they combined his old-world style with your modern flare is stunning."

She wasn't wrong. Beneath the herring bone-lined bodice was a cobalt tunic dress with flowy sleeves that fell off my shoulders. It would have shown off a healthy dose of cleavage, if I had any to speak of. As it was, Mics had to use bronzer to create the illusion of boobs.

After screwing the cap back on the gloss, I dropped it to the vanity counter and met Micah's gaze in the mirror. "War is raging all around, and here we are fighting it one fashion trend at a time."

"Sometimes all it takes to flame the desire to rebel is a spark of hope held up from amidst the masses." Thumbs looped in the pockets of his brown-tweed suit coat, the deep timbre of Vlad's cadence rumbled from the doorway of the green room. "And, sometimes, that spark is a fetching pair of boots."

Whoever dressed the Prince of Darkness deserved a fruit basket, and a high-five. His suit fit him like a second skin, showcasing his broad chest before tapering down his sculpted torso. The blue of his tie perfectly matched my dress, tying our looks together with orchestrated ease.

"Look at that," my words morphed into a grunt as Micah yanked at the laces once more, "the man's got jokes."

The corners of Vlad's sea-foam green eyes crinkled into a charming grin. "My apologies for the interruption. Renfield suggested I come to be ... how did he put it? *Prepped* for the interview. I don't know if that is actually something of critical importance, but he was quite insistent. Personally, I think it's his diet that makes him so ... intense. Did you know he only allows himself one drop of blood per day? He says that's how he controls the lure of his hunger."

One mystery solved, I slapped my hand to the Formica countertop. "*That's* why he looks like a dried stick of jerky! He's like an undead Gandhi!"

"Prepping is a *fantastic* idea," Micah silenced me with a sideways glare. "You two need to convince the world you're in love. Don't lie about how you met, use the real story. After that, if it helps, think of the greatest love of your life and play off of that."

"My ex slaughtered my entire family while I watched."

"My wife died in my arms." Vlad lobbed back with a nod of understanding.

Micah's shoulders sagged. "Just look at each other like the sun rises and sets on the other's ass, and you'll be fine. Now, I'm going to go get a status update on any breaking news stories. The last thing we need is to get blindsided on air."

An awkward silence settling between us, Vlad and I watched Micah disappear down the hall. It seemed so much easier to play off each other when we had an audience. Albeit, a reluctant one.

Checking my appearance in the mirror one last time, my gaze drew to Vlad with a magnetic tug. "I know it's our job to sell this whole *happily ever after* scenario. But, I need you to know I'm not a stage-five clinger."

A deep V of confusion creased his forehead. "I'm unclear of the meaning behind that sentiment."

Turning my back to the mirror, I leaned one hip against the vanity. "I felt I needed to make it clear that I know we are each playing a part. We can go in front of the cameras and pledge our love for each other, but that doesn't make any of it real. I just … didn't want you to think I was under the confused notion there was something here that isn't."

Gliding across the room, Vlad edged up beside me. Lips parted with naughty promise, he leaned in, leaving nothing but a thin veil of sparking energy between us.

"In my day," his gaze leisurely traveled the length of me, taking the time to round the curves. "Arranged marriages were a common place occurrence. They were set up for the benefit of families and title. While they weren't instigated by the sweet song birds of love, that doesn't mean deep thralls of passion didn't bloom between the united couple." Dragging his stare to mine, his seductive smile caused waves of longing to ripple through me. "Of course, back then I would have been paid a dowry of some sort—a few sheep, or pigs—in case such a bond never formed."

"The sandwich wraps on the Kraft service table have bacon on them," I offered in a throaty whisper. "Does that count?"

Vlad bit his lower lip, trying unsuccessfully to squelch a grin. "No pork offerings are needed." Tracing his knuckle down the length of my arm, he laced his fingers with mine. The sharp chill of his skin sent shivers jolting through my breasts. "You stated your stance. Now hear mine. I do not take vows of any kind lightly. When I make a pledge to you, it will be done of heart, body, and soul."

"Wow," Wetting my suddenly parched lips, I gently pulled back to extract my fingers from his. "Dracula's got game."

"Game?"

"You know what the ladies like." At a loss of what to do with my hands, I smoothed them over the fabric of my bodice.

Knuckle curled beneath my chin, Vlad tipped my face to his. Breathing his words into me, his lips teased over mine without the sweet gratification of touch. "My beautiful queen, I don't *got game.* I *invented* the game." Without another word, he turned on his heel and sauntered from the room, pausing only to throw a come-and-get-me look over his shoulder. "I'll see you on set. Don't keep me waiting."

Micah, who had watched the entire exchange from the doorway, side stepped to allow him to pass.

Mouth falling open, I gaped her way at a dumbfounded loss. "*Son of a bitch,*" I managed. "I am *so* out of my league."

Craning her neck, Mics sought a second glimpse of his butt. "Damn right you are."

EIGHTEEN

VINX

Vlad and I sat side by side on a stiff beige couch; legs touching, and fingers intertwined. An arrangement of white hydrangeas decorated the walnut coffee table positioned in front of us. Every bit of the set was designed to look like someone's cozy living room. It would have been far more welcoming if cameras and lights weren't boring into us from every angle imaginable.

Michelle Hutson, an attractive middle-aged reporter with shoulder-length chestnut hair and an inquisitive stare, crossed her legs at the ankle and shuffled the order of her notecards. "No one can deny you're a stunning couple. Tell me, how much truth is there in the rumor that, Vlad, you tasted Vincenza's blood and fell in love? And if so, what do you say to skeptics that believe this whole romantic tale is meant to distract from more volatile Nosferatu matters?"

Playing his part with theatrical brilliance, Vlad's head dipped with a sheepish grin. "If we were truly trying to sell a fairytale, I wager we would leave out what happened after I woke. That part was far from tender."

As I patted his knee with our joined fingers, I gazed up at him with loving adoration. "I was the latest initiate of the Court—"

"Can you explain to our viewers what exactly that is?"

"It would be my pleasure." Tossing my tousled bob, I offered Michelle a camera-ready smile. "It's an elite counsel that oversees all broad scoping Nosferatu matters, such as the recent epidemic of attacks and hate crimes."

Index finger pressed to her lips, Michelle frowned and shook her head. "Such a horrible ordeal." In a blink, silver sparks of interest brightened her eyes, and her posture changed from professional to sassy girlfriend. "So, your initiation into this club was with something called a bloodsharing?"

Swallowing my annoyance, I kept my grin plastered in place. "It was. On each full moon the Court gathers for a sacramental bloodsharing over Vlad's resting place. I let a couple of drops fall, and found out the hard way he is *definitely* not a morning person."

"I bit her." Vlad grimaced, ever the sexy, naughty boy. "In my defense, I was out of my mind from starvation and solitude."

"Nothing was done that couldn't be undone with a band-aid and an apology." Playfully, I bumped his elbow with mine.

Turning his face from the cameras, he peered down at me with a focused intensity that made my belly flipflop. "I would chain myself in silver before ever harming my future queen again."

"How does it feel to hear that title out loud, Vincenza?" Michelle slid to the edge of her chair, careful to keep her good side to the viewing public. "Are you ready to be Lady Draculesti, Queen of the Nosferatu?"

Puffing my cheeks, I pantomimed blowing out a breath through pursed lips. "Can anyone ever be ready for that kind of thing? I'm just a girl from Connecticut that met a guy, and fell in love. Whatever comes next, we'll figure out … together."

"Yes, these are troubled time. Watching a fairytale play out is a welcome distraction from the ugliness we are assaulted with daily." Back straightening, as if fearing her interview was getting to cutesy, Michelle's almond-shaped eyes narrowed. "Which brings me to my next question. You mentioned the recent rash of Nosferatu attacks. You were in that airplane hangar when Vlad's son, Rau Mihnea, allegedly murdered a young woman. At this very moment, there is a nationwide manhunt for him in the United States. Tell me, Vincenza, having witnessed Rau's crimes, do your and Vlad's views differ on the charges against him?"

This was it. The moment I could plant the seed of truth and begin nurturing it. "I *was* in that airplane hangar. I saw what happened, and what is *continuing* to happen. Rau is suffering from a sickness, and he's not the only one. This virus is similar to rabies, and it is what's causing vampires to act out in violent ways. These vampires do not need to be imprisoned or killed. They need *treatment*."

"As a family," Vlad added his voice to our mutual stance, "we want to get my boy home, so that we may begin the hunt for a cure. Not for him alone, but countless others that are inflicted."

My fangs threatened when I realized Michelle wasn't even pretending to listen. She pressed two fingers to her ear piece, listening to a message from the control room. Turning her face from the cameras, she muttered into her mic, "We don't do that. This isn't some public access channel. It's prime time." A beat passed as she listened to their response. "Because, *Stephen*, it makes us look like a second-rate show. No, threats aren't necessary. Just patch the fucking thing through." Glancing up, her bright smile returned as if nothing had happened. "It seems we have a caller with a question."

Feeling Vlad tense beside me, I ignored the internal screaming in my mind and gushed on both our behalves, "What a fun surprise!"

"We're patching them through now." Michelle nodded, taking direction from the voice in her ear. "Caller, you are on with Vlad Draculesti and Vincenza Larow. What question did you have for them?"

A moment of static, then a slick voice filled the studio. "Vlad, old friend, it's been a long time."

105

One syllable uttered from that silky cadence and my vision tunneled.

Tendrils of evil snaked into my veins, binding me to the chair.

I couldn't move.

Couldn't think … not of anything more than my reoccurring nightmares.

… thank you, my dark lords, for helping me. May you make the cord between myself and Vincenza strong like the chains … of a prisoner.

"Dorian!" Features sharpening with a dangerous edge, Vlad sprang from his seat. "Show yourself, you villainous rat!"

"You'd like that, wouldn't you?" Dorian chuckled, ice clinking in a glass on the other side of the line. "For me to show my true face to the world, as you have?"

The red lights from the cameras flicked off.

Everyone, except Vlad and myself, stood frozen stone still—a room full of statues.

Imprisoned inside my own body, blood tinged tears streaked my cheeks. The jagged hint of a memory dug, clawed, and licked at the wall of my mind, desperate to be remembered.

Hands curling into tight fists, Vlad's eyes blinked to reptilian slits. His fangs elongated into a vicious maw, saliva dripping from their deadly points. "What do you want, Gray? Speak, you squirming larva!"

"I want to talk about this little stunt of yours." Ice clinked once more, as if Dorian was rolling it around the edges of a glass. "You know, the one where you become the relatable hero to the people?"

Vlad's head tilted with a serpent-like roll of his neck. "Fearful of having a little competition in front of the masses?"

"From *you?*" Dorian erupted in hearty peals of laughter. "You have many strengths, old friend. Being charismatic under pressure has *never* been one of them. No, I'm contacting you to deliver a public service announcement. Look around, Vlad. Do you see those glassy-eyed stares peering back at you? *That* is my doing. I need not be present to have them all under my control."

Throwing his head back, Vlad shouted at the ceiling. "Once more you're hiding behind parlor tricks. *You coward*!"

"A trick, is it? Many things have changed since you retreated into hiding. Perhaps you need a sampling of how my powers have grown?"

With an audible snap of Dorian's fingers, a heavy-set crew member—with mustard stains on the front of his flannel shirt--stepped out from behind the camera. Pulling an ink pen from his breast pocket, he rolled it over his fingers into a tight fist. Then, without a second of hesitation, he plunged it hard and fast into his right eye. Blood spurt from the wound, streaking the man's face in a current of gore. Seemingly oblivious to the Bic jutting from his eye socket, the crew member returned to stone stillness.

Vlad sniffed the air once, then again, his pupils dilating with hunger.

"Look at how you twitch!" Dorian laughed. "Then again, aren't we all victims to our own appetites? Mine, is for war. You denied me it once, Draculesti. Going so far as to hide away my very favorite toy … *you*. Have no fear, since then I've been planning, plotting, and eagerly awaiting your return. At long last, the time has come. With this little *display*," he spat the word as if it were beneath him, "comes a message. Consider this a small sampling. One that motivates you to shake out your joints, and knock off the rust from your slumber. Because, I need you at full strength for what's to come."

A click, and the call ended, awakening bedlam in the studio.

Screams rang out.

Visibly trembling, Michelle called 911.

Vlad shook off his vampiric attributes, and bolted to the cameraman's side at the same instant the man slumped to the floor in shock. Rolling him onto his back, Vlad plucked the pen from his socket, causing discharge to pulse from the wound. Two other crew members ran to help their fallen friend, only to pull up short and heave at the sight of his injury.

Not trusting himself to drop fang so close to an injured human, Vlad bit the inside of his wrist with his human teeth, gnawing until he tore through to a claret gush. Unceremoniously, he forced his wrist to the cameraman's lips.

"Vampire blood is finicky and unpredictable," he rumbled to the two green-hued aids. "There's no telling if this will save his sight, yet it should spare him the gaping hole in his skull." Satisfied with how much of his blood his patient ingested, Vlad clapped his opposite hand over his wrist and rose to his feet. "Stay with him until help arrives."

Striding to where I still sat in stunned confusion, Vlad hooked me by the elbow and dragged me to my feet.

"The cameraman will be fine," he muttered against my ear, rushing me from the mayhem.

World moving in a dizzying blur, I peered up at Vlad, struck once more by the tragic poetry of his beauty. "That voice." I slurred, tongue thick and heavy. "I've heard it before. Who was that?"

Bursting out the side door into the brisk chill of night, Vlad's wild eyes appeared—*dare I say it?*—scared. "That … was the Prince of Chaos."

NINETEEN
VLAD

King Corvinus lounged on his throne, eating a plum and licking its dripping juices off the side of his hand. With his double chin, gold embroidered robes, and powder-soft skin it appeared a full day's hard labor was something this man never experienced. The platinum wig he wore sat slightly askew, just enough to be noticeable.

Despite being announced before him, he still purposely kept me waiting. Hands clasped behind my back, I shifted my weight from one foot to the other and struggled not to take this as a bad omen. Only after finishing every bit of the decadent fruit, and wiping his hands clean on a cloth offered by a footman, did he bother to glance my way.

"Vlad Draculesti," he boomed, his voice echoing through the cavernous throne room. "You're a bold man for coming before me after stealing Jusztina's hand, without *bothering* to ask my blessing.

Have you any idea the life I had planned for her? As part of my peace treaty with Frederick III, she was to wed his nephew. That simpleton was so eager for the union he agreed to pay *me* a handsome dowry for arranging it. All was set, and arranged. Then, you snuck in like a fox in a chicken coop, and whisked her away. I assume you've come to apologize?"

"I love Jusztina, Your Highness. For *that*, I will never apologize." Nostrils flaring, the king bristled, prompting an immediate retraction on my part. "However, I *will* admit that my actions were ill-mannered. Her being a descendent of royal blood, I should have honored you by acquiring your blessing."

"*Yes, you should have.*" Spitting the words in a barely contained fury foamy spittle gathered in the corners of Corvinus's mouth. "After such insult, you have the gall to come before me? Why am I being forced to look upon you? *Speak!*"

At the king's rage, armored guards crept from the shadows, lining the perimeter of the cathedral. Fingers twitching toward my sword, I felt the icy chill of awareness that The Dragon remained silent. No churning darkness squirmed within. No red haze of wrath seeped around the edges of my vision. In fact, since Dorian muzzled *Drákon*, I had felt no stirrings from him at all.

I was truly and utterly alone.

A perplexing state of affairs given my current situation.

Sensing this wasn't going to end well, my hand drifted toward my sword. Fingers closing around the hilt, I kept it at my hip … for now. "I've come because I see the love you have for your family. You are a good and benevolent king, and would never want any harm to come to them. Right now, Jusztina is in great danger. As are the people of Transylvania."

Leaning back in his throne, Corvinus rubbed his palms over the arm rests. "Yet here you are, *brave hero*, having left them behind to save yourself."

"Only to beseech your aid. The Ottoman Empire and Saxons are threatening—"

"That's what they do," Corvinus chuckled, thoroughly enjoying my agitation. "They attack, and seize what they want by brutal, unforgiving means. I heard the worst of it came when their army was led by a man they referred to as The Impaler. But, you wouldn't know anything about that, would you?"

Biting back a sharp rebuttal, I battled to keep my tone calm and measured. "Your Majesty, if they find Jusztina—"

The king slouched to the side, attempting to shrivel me with a victorious smirk. "*When* they find her, they won't harm one hair on her pretty little head. Because, you see, those were the terms we agreed upon when they came here … *for my consent.*"

Top lip curling into a snarl, I freed my sword with a deadly hiss. "Lies! You're a Christian. Even you couldn't be so foul!" I bellowed.

The guards drew their weapons in response, gazes locked on their king in anticipation of his signal to attack.

Fortunately, Corvinus wasn't done rubbing my nose in his betrayal. "The Catholic Church has offered no substantial aid to my reign. An oversight The Ottoman Empire was *eager* to remedy. I found their donation generous enough to rethink my policies against them. They *were* meant to kill you, finally freeing Jusztina for a suitable marriage. That said, I think it will be *far* more fun to imprison you for life. You can rot there, knowing your precious love is in the arms of another."

The king leaned forward with his elbows on his knees, and jerked one finger at his men.

Leaping to action, they charged.

The steel of my sword met that of another in an ear-piercing clang. I struck and blocked with all of my might, all for naught. Without The Dragon, I was no match for their numbers.

TWENTY

VINX

With Vlad holding tight to my elbow, we burst out of the television studio at a sprint. Bile scorched up the back of my throat, tears burning behind my eyes.

"Stop," I managed in a barely audible whisper. "Please, Vlad. I need ... I have to ..."

My words failed to register with the vampire king. Features set in a determined scowl, his eyes were glowing rubies of destruction.

"Vlad? Can we just ..." Planting my feet, I pulled against him with all my might. "Stop, damn it!"

Snapped from his grim reverie, he spun to face me. "We can't stop. We have to move."

Yanking my arm away, I refused to budge. "No! Not until you tell me what the fuck that was? I mean, that guy *jabbed a pen in his own eye*! Who has the power to make a person do that? You know what?

113

No. On second thought, save it. I don't want to hear it. Because, you need to realize that what just happened in there?" Jabbing my thumb in the direction of the studio, I dropped fang in open challenge. "It's on you. You have all this strength and ability, yet refuse to use it! Our enemies are coming at us with everything they've got, and you won't unleash our one and only weapon—*you!*"

In a blink, his more beastly attributes vanished. Chased away by blatant sorrow. Rooted where he stood, he extended his hand to me palm up. "Come with me. It's time for you to learn the truth."

"About *what?*" I hollered, wanting nothing more than to grab him by the shoulders and shake his mountain of secrets out of him.

"About who it is we are up against, and why we should all be terrified."

"SAY THE NAME Dracula and people respond with shivers of anticipation. The myth, legends, and lore paint me as a god, simply because I was the first. The reality is, I was little more than the earliest infected by the Nosferatu disease. Meanwhile, utterances of Vlad the Impaler garner a far different response." Having whisked us back to Castle Dracul in a rolling fog, Vlad pushed aside a bookcase to reveal stone stairs leading down to a pitch-black tunnel.

"Not everyone," I corrected, flicking on the flash light setting on my phone. "Those busts of you throughout Transylvania tell the story of a group of people that view you a hero. Quick question, where are we? Because this kinda has a 'Hallway to Your Kill Room' feel to it."

"Nothing like that. This is the route to my secret dungeon."

"So, by nothing like that you meant *exactly* like that. Got it." Walking through a spiderweb, I did a full body shiver to shake it off.

Vlad stopped outside of a wrought iron gate. Pulling a skeleton key from his breast pocket, he unlocked it. "Not a day passes that I don't bless the people of Transylvania for remembering me with kindness." The gate opened with a shriek of protest, inviting us into a closet-sized cell reeking of dirt and stale air. In the center of the room, carefully polished and cared for, hung an artistry of armor. The arm plates gleamed a brilliant silver, the chest stained a deep crimson. Every joint was riveted with gold, the leather binding straps freshly oiled.

My mind traveled back to the march in Washington and the artifacts of Vlad's on display. "Was this your original armor? There is one, pressed with your seal, that makes the rounds at public events."

"I would wager what you saw was my formal plating for parades and gatherings. Nothing more than decoration, really. This, however," tongue clucking against the roof of his mouth, Vlad gazed upon the armor with tangible appreciation, "was a part of me, for quite some time."

Leaning one shoulder against the rough face of the stone wall, I studied the mythical marvel before me. "Tell me about it?"

"When my heart still beat as a mortal man, this armor protected me in the most fierce of battles. See this mark, here?" He pointed to a nick in the lower left quadrant of the metal, no more than an inch in length. "That happened on a battle field in Turkey. A soldier leapt off his horse, hoping to drive his sword straight into my kidney. And this?" His fingers danced over a chip at the neck line, right below where his jugular would have been. "I challenged four men at once. One nearly claimed my head as a prize. Without this well-crafted iron, I would have died a hundred times over." He fell silent for a moment, the expression that stole over his features bordering on wistful. Jerking himself from the trance of what might have been, he cast a quizzical glance in my direction. "Have you ever watched the intricate artform of armor being crafted?"

I shook my head no, Vlad responding in turn with a nod of understanding.

"The iron is heated over a fire stoked so hot it instantly scorches the skin, if the proper protective leathers aren't worn. Then, it's painstakingly hammered and molded into the ideal shape." Fingertips dragging over the dragon stamped into the metal, Vlad peered at the armor like an ally he would lay down his life for. "That perfect shape saves lives, and wins battles."

While cold didn't bother me as it once did, a chill from our chosen topic prompted goosebumps to sprout on my arms. "No doubt that would breed a sentimental attachment to it."

"It's so much more than that," Vlad traced over every rivet. "This iron shell protected me from the world. While the room we're standing in protected the world ... from me."

Glancing over his shoulder, he caught my stare and dragged it to the wall behind me.

Head swiveling, I let him steer my attention to heavy shackles chained to the stone floor, and a tapestry of a claw marks sliced into the stone. "Wha—what is that?"

"That," a sad smile tugged back one corner of his mouth, "is your introduction to *Drákon*, the entity that made me what I am."

Squatting down to inspect the markings, I poked my index finger into one of the crevices. At its deepest, it dug in up to my first knuckle. "How were these marks made?"

"History believes him to be a demon." Assuming a wide-legged stance, he shoved his hands into the pockets of his suit coat. "I was never satisfied with that titling. Demons are easily vanquished. *Drákon's* level of benevolence seems far more ... eternal."

Hanging on his every word, I wet my arid lips. "If not a demon, what was he?"

Edging up beside me, shoulder brushing mine, Vlad eyed the lace work pattern of gouges. "I cannot say for sure. Yet, I believe him to be the very root of all evil. Every demented act committed in the world. Every twisted thought pondered. It all spawns from The Dragon. It's the vile whisper at the back of our minds, tempting and taunting us into deplorable acts. It was the nails hammered into Christ on the cross. The snake that slithered through the Garden of Eden. Cain's motivation for killing Abel. It was because of Dorian Gray, the man who overtook the studio tonight, that I had no choice but to submit to that malevolent crux."

Dropping my arm, I linked my hand with Vlad's in a show of solidarity. "You took on The Dragon, and became the first of our kind. If we are all descendants of you—and what you believe of The Dragon is fact—that would make us exactly the evil beasts those bigots on the TV accuse us of being. I refuse to accept that. I've seen humans commit unspeakable acts, while vampires behave selflessly. And vice versa. I can't wrap my mind around any version of this that reduces an entire faction of people down to one binding label."

Vlad peered down at our intertwined fingers. With a bend of his elbow, he turned them over in fascinated inspection. "The strength and attributes of my curse I have passed along to our kind. The Dragon is mine alone to bear. He chose me. Roosts only in me. Dorian summoned it, and sought to take it on himself. To his dismay, it selected me. Through the years I've tried to cast it out. It seems as long as it deems me worthy, I shall harbor its burden alone."

"While you continue to hate yourself for it."

"My own vessel is the only armor we truly have against that serpent of darkness. I can subdue the beast to some degree, but if it ... no, *I* ... were ever to lose control, you musn't try to save me." Gathering both my hands in his, he pressed them to the haunting stillness of his chest. "Were that to happen, promise you won't try to save me. Run fast. Run far. *Never* look back. Swear that to me."

Feeling as if the walls were closing in under the weight of his ominous warning, I tried to extract my fingers from his vise grip hold. "Look, I hate to poke a *literal* sleeping dragon here, but couldn't that be *exactly* what we need? My brother. Your son. All those people being killed and enslaved. We could just ... you know ... turn you loose and adopt that run like hell philosophy. You would be like our fanged grenade."

Lips pressed in a thin line, Vlad knelt beside the shackles on the floor. Picking one up, he weighed it in his palm. "You would be replacing one monster with another. I wouldn't stop at our enemies. My thirst would rage until sated. That is exactly what Dorian wants. *This* is why he is provoking me. With nothing to gain from this, he craves only the chaos of war. How do you fight someone with nothing to lose?"

'Is this why you brought me here? To prove it's already over?" Hands on my hips, I shook my head. "No, I don't accept that."

'There may be another way." Vlad discarded the shackles to the floor with a *clank*, and rose to his feet. "Dorian's mortality is tied to an enchanted portrait of himself. Were it in our possession, we may have a way to weaken him. Or, at the very least, a bargaining chip to use in our favor."

'The all-powerful warlock's greatest weakness is a bad selfie? And people say the millennials are bad."

Rubbing his hands together, Vlad wiped off the lingering residue from the chains. "My resources are plentiful. I can have my men search the farthest reaches of the world to find that painting. In the meantime, I suggest we continue the plans for our nuptials. It will keep his attention focused on us, and away from our search efforts. Not to mention, we've already seen how it agitates him. It could benefit us to keep him off kilter."

'What if we can't find it?" Dreading his answer, I chewed on the inside of my cheek.

Shrinking back into the shadows of the cell, darkness stretched and rolled around Vlad's silhouette, eager to consume him. "Then, we brace for the battle to come."

TWENTY-ONE

VINX

Vlad said we.

We will brace for the battle to come.

Bleak as our circumstances were, I was choosing to cling to the glimmer of hope that he was slowly being swayed toward standing with us. Eager to share this news with the others, my hand was closing around the doorknob to my bedroom when it was yanked out of my grip from a hand on the other side.

Chest rising and falling in frantic pants, Carter's brow dripped with sweat. "Vincenza! There you are! I've been looking all over for you."

"And here *you* are. Alone in my room. Like a creeper. *Again.*"

If he heard the judgement in my tone, Carter ignored it. Launching forward, he grabbed me in a bear hug, squeezing me with bone crushing urgency. Given our sudden intimate proximity, I couldn't help but notice his entire body seemed to be vibrating.

"Micah told us what happened at the studio, she got a ride back with Vlad's people." The word's poured from his lips in a gushing spigot, showing no signs of slowing or stopping. "Have you seen some of those guys? Dressed in normal suits they look like the undead secret service. Mics said some cameraman jammed a pen in his eye. Is that true? Why would anyone do that? After that, everyone started looking for you. No one had any idea where you disappeared to, and crazy panic ensued. How did you get back, by the way? It doesn't matter. I'm just so glad you're here and you're safe. You'll probably get a major tongue lashing from Mics, though. The vamp she had to sit next to during the car ride home is on a special diet where he can only tolerate the blood of minks, ferrets, and weasels. Be prepared to hear all about his musky odor." Finally pulling back, his spastically twitching stare bounced from one spot on my face to another, never settling. "Are you okay? Why aren't you saying anything?"

"Mostly because I'm waiting for you to pause and take a breath," I marveled, eyes wide and unblinking. "What the hell, man? You are *literally* buzzing."

Running circles around us, Batdog yipped and snorted in an urgent demand to be scooped up and loved on. While I wanted to oblige my wriggly little pooch, I hesitated out of concern for having to catch Carter if he crashed from whatever this was.

Carter folded his hands in a prayer pose, and pressed them tight to his chest. "*I know.* It's weird, right? There was a bottle of wine left in my room. I enjoy a good Bordeaux as much as the next guy, so I treated myself to a glass. That led to me finishing the entire bottle. Now, I'm thinking Romanian wine is laced with caffeine or crack. Because, my ears are ringing, and I can't decide if I want to run a marathon or take a nap. It changes from second to second." Carter's cheeks puffed as he expelled a breath through pursed lips. Stumbling back, he flopped down on the edge of my bed. "Whoa, crushing exhaustion moment. You talk now."

Scooping up my pup, I accepted his shower of sloppy kisses as I strode to the night stand to hand Carter the glass of water I kept there. "Maybe stick to water for the rest of the day."

His hands quaked as he brought the glass to his lips, sloshing drops over the rim.

"So, want to tell me what really happened today?" he asked, after successfully managing to force down a gulp.

Slapping at his knee, I urged Carter to scoot over then sank onto the mattress beside him. Kicking off my heels, I curled my legs under me. "An old enemy of Vlad's, Dorian something, was behind today's assault. Apparently, he has a *ridiculous* amount of black magic. The two have bad blood that dates back centuries. The guy wanted to coax Vlad's darker side out to play. But, I was with him the entire time and—as far as I could tell—he never came close to letting it slip. Either the part of himself Vlad lives in fear of is buried too deep, or he has *way* better control than he gives himself credit for."

"Is that a bit of affection I hear developing in your tone?" Carter reached past me to set the water on the end table.

"Are you seriously asking me if I have a crush on the guy you *all* arranged for me to marry? *Really?*"

"That's not a denial."

Hopping off my lap, Batdog spun in three circles before sinking down into a cozy spot.

"He's a god among men in the literal sense of the term. How could I not find him fascinating?" I paused long enough to gauge Carter's reaction, part of me secretly thrilled when he bristled. "I also find him *incredibly* intimidating. Then, of course, there's the multi-generational gap between us. He's mystified by indoor plumbing, while I'm bummed the wifi isn't better here." That part was a blatant lie. Vlad drank blood from those of us accustomed to the modern world, which allowed him to integrate with ease. Still, that wasn't what Carter needed to hear. "Truth is, other than fangs, we have nothing in common.

Struck by another wave of his jittery high, he leapt off the bed and hurled himself into a series of jumping jacks. "How did the *god among men* think we should handle his arch-nemesis? Please tell me it involved finding Markus and mailing parts of him back to this Dorian guy in tiny gift-wrapped boxes."

It was on the tip of my tongue to reveal Vlad's plan of searching for Dorian's painting. It was Carter's extreme vulnerability as a human amongst vampires and warlocks that held me back. If Dorian could coerce someone into stabbing themselves simply to make a point, what measures would he take to get information out of a breakable mortal?

Clamping down on that bit of information, I leaned back on my elbow and dragged one hand through my hair. "He suggested we keep on track to wedded bliss."

Carter dropped to the floor, pumping out a series of push-ups. "Of course he did," he bitterly grunted in between reps.

"Has there been any more footage of Jeremy?" Rolling onto my stomach, I peeked over the edge of the mattress to see the bands of muscles across Carter's back straining against the fabric of his shirt. "Did he look all right? No visible signs that they're hurting him?"

Jet over, Carter bounced to his feet, only to stumble and reel as if the world was spinning. "Okay, it wasn't crack in that wine. It was LSD. You mentioned Jeremy, and *poof*. He's in the mirror, staring back at me. I'm officially straight-up tripping balls." Hunching his shoulders, he waved at his hallucination. "Hi there, my freaky little mind fuck! Thanks so much for stopping by!"

"Uh, hi?" the mirror responded.

Leaping to my feet, I dropped fang and spun toward the full-length mirror. All battle instincts faded, floating away on a breeze, the second I saw the familiar face peering back at me with a sardonic smile.

"Hey, sis. Good to see ya." Jeremy grinned, as if time, and death, hadn't separated us.

"Jer?" Legs threatening to buckle, I steadied myself against the bedpost.

Carter's shoulders sank with relief. "Oh, good. You can see him, too! So happy I'm not trippin'. Last time I did shrooms I got kicked out of Dairy Queen for getting to second base with their Blizzard display." At my quizzical glance, he added, "I licked it. A lot. *Obscene* amount of tongue."

Holding up one finger, I halted any further details of *that* particular disturbing backstory. "We are going to move past that, and vow *never* to speak of it again." Turning my attention back to the mirror, I floated forward, drawn by the improbable. "How? How is this possible?"

Jeremy's head listed to the side, one brow hitching in amusement. "Said the girl who came back from the dead, to her brother that managed to do the same. Is it just the mirror part boggling your mind, genius?"

Reaching out, my fingertips found the cool face of the glass. I traced the outline of his face in desperation to commit him to memory—alive and well. "Are you okay? I swear to Vlad I will kill anyone that harms one hair on your—"

Jeremy glanced to the right of him, as if worried someone was coming, then held up one hand to silence me. "Vinx, I don't have much time, but I had to warn you." His image began to falter, flickering in and out of focus. "This big public show you're ... putting on with Vlad? Dorian ... doesn't like it."

Slapping my hands to the glass to get better reception, I blatantly ignored the fact that made no damned sense. "Jer? *Stay with me*! I love you!"

As the image dwindled to nothingness, I fought to piece together my brother's pivotal caveat. "Dorian ... coming for Vlad. If ... in the way ... go down with him. Run, Vinx ... no idea what he is capable of."

TWENTY-TWO

VLAD

What do you think will become of your sweet Jusztina now? Drákon's demonic hiss trumpeted through my mind with stabbing intensity. His return provided proof that Dorian hadn't suppressed him as I thought. Not permanently anyway. Instead, it seemed he chose to lay dormant, waiting for the perfect opportunity to exploit my weakness to its full extent. *Meanwhile, here you sit—the noble hero, who threw his sweet little lamb to the wolves thirsting for his blood.*

"Stop it!" Swinging into a strike, I pounded my fist into one jagged stone wall of the dungeon cell that held me. The knuckle of my middle fingers cracked open, skin peeling back in an angry gash. "Leave me alone!"

"Enough of that! Settle down." Hollered Corvinus's guard stationed at the door, shifting the heavy weight of his armored physique from one foot to the other.

"You could have helped!" I screamed my throat raw at The Dragon, completely ignoring such a pointless thing as the guard's command. "You could have gotten us out of here!"

Face reddening to match his auburn beard, the guard slammed his sword against the iron bars with a deafening *clang*. "You will be silent, or I will silence you!"

Help? My dark passenger purred for my ears only. *After all I've done you still desire more?*

"All you've done?" I repeated with a humorless laugh that bordered on manic. "*You've made me a monster!*"

"Last warning, boy!" Keys jangling, the guard searched for the right one to unlock my cell from the plethora of those strung to his belt with a leather string.

I gave you power. Prestige. Reputation. Drákon boasted. *Everything you have is thanks to me. Still, you seek more without offering anything in return.*

"What you want I cannot give," I sobbed at my own ineptitude, shoulders sagging.

The guard's hand fell away from the keys with a brief nod of approval. "That's it, lad. Just settle."

Snaking from one ear to the other, The Dragon's voice shifted all around. *Ah, but you can. Drink of the sacrament. Secure our bond that we may be one at long last.*

"Please, no," I pleaded, fearing for the only thing I had left to lose—my soul. "Take my body. Do with it as you will. I merely ask that you not demand of that which I cannot give, as my soul belongs to Christ."

The guard glanced over his shoulder, undoubtably praying no one heard that. "I ... never asked for your body. No need to spread that bit of rubbish around."

If you want to save Jusztina, and the people of Transylvania, the bond must be forged. No further allowances will be granted.

"No," I whimpered, head shaking in defeat.

They will save her for last, after they've burned the entire village while she is made to watch. How do you think her sweet spirit will fair after such turmoil?

Chin falling to my chest, I loathed myself for stammering out the words that would condemn me for all eternity. "W-what ... will you have me d-do?"

Blood, the word rattled through my core, winding through my veins with the vile awareness of what must be done. *It completes the bond.*

Closing my hands in prayer, I sought out the Lord to protect me from this damning temptation. *"Our Father, Who art in heaven, hallowed be Thy name: Thy kingdom come: Thy will be done on earth as it is in heaven."*

Yesssss, call out to Him, The Dragon snickered. *I'm sure He'll come bursting in to save a man who has taken so many lives with such grand flourish.*

Shaking his head in aggravation, the guard stuck the key in the lock. "We're going to get you in shackles and to a priest. I'm not prepared to handle one speaking in tongues."

"No! Stay back!" Stabbing one hand out to halt him, I frantically resumed my prayer vigil. "Give us this day our daily bread; and forgive us our trespasses as we forgive those who trespass against us."

To my great regret, the lock clicked, and the gate swung open. The instant the guard stepped inside, I could smell the heady tonic of his blood calling to me. Saliva filling my mouth, I fixated on the thick vein of life pulsing at the side of his neck. I squeezed my eyes shut, fighting the lure the only way I could. "And lead us not into temptation, but deliver us from evil."

"Hold out your hands." Shackles dangling from his thumb, the guard waved me closer. "We need to get you restrained."

Unimaginable power will be yours to wield. You will be ... unstoppable.

Scrambling back, my shoulder blades slammed into the wall. *"Stop! I beg of you!"*

"Easy now." Freehand poised in front of him, the guard risked another step closer.

Act out of love for your wife, and people, Drákon urged, talking directly to my slipping resolve. *How could that be wrong?*

"There now, that's a good lad." Opening the shackles, the guard reached for my wrists.

I let myself slump in his direction, breathing in the appetizing allure of his aroma.

"Sorry for the weight of these, friend." The guard grunted, fiddling to clasp the first shackle into place. "These are for your safety as much as mine."

"T'is I that am truly sorry." The decision was made as I uttered those fateful words. Lips peeling from my teeth, I lunged.

I knew not what I was doing, had no weapon to speak of. Like a rabid animal, foaming and snarling, I went for his throat. Chomping down with dull, human teeth, I ripped my way through meat and tendons. As my head flung from side to side, I felt the sickening pops of tearing flesh. The hot rush of coppery warmth flooded my mouth, gushing down my chin. Its metallic taste gagged me at first swallow. Earsplitting screams rang in my ears. Lips locked around the bubbling flow, I alternated between ravenous pulls and stomach lurching heaves.

I rode the guard's body to the ground, not loosening my hold until his lifeless eyes stared up at the ceiling. His mouth forever frozen in a silent scream. Throat hanging open in a gaping maw of shredded tissue, blood spread around him in a growing pool.

Palms slapping against the slick floor, I pushed myself as far from the carnage as my miniscule cell would allow. What started as tremors morphed into spastic convulsions that rippled through me, jarring my bones to their marrow. "*What ... have ... I ... done?*"

You secured our bond, slave. The Dragon's voice came more crisp and clear than ever before, puffs of its breath tickling down my spine. *As I always knew you would.*

I whipped around, fully expecting the beast to have manifested behind me.

Nonetheless, I found myself alone with my sin.

"You told me you would help me save Jusztina!" I shouted at the blood streaked walls closing in. "*What happens now?*"

Now? Amusement twined through *Drákon's* hellish whisper. *Dear boy, now you … die.*

The instant he uttered the word, my heart seized in my chest. Unable to draw a breath, I clawed at my throat, dots swimming before my eyes. Sinking to the ground, the black steed of death rode in to claim me.

TWENTY-THREE

VINX

Perched, once more, on the bathroom countertop, I kept my eyes closed while Micah brushed eye shadow over my lids. My outfit for yet another day of publicity spots was a forest green cowl-necked sweater belted at the waist, tawny colored leggings, and ankle boots. The front of my chin-length bob had been braided at my temples and pinned back, the rest curled into a crown of messy tendrils.

"I know you love your brother, but adhering to the warning of a mysterious figure in a mirror isn't really an option." Micah stated. Standing back, she inspected her work only to add a bit more color to my left eye. "Trust me, if that Dorian person has the power to cause self-mutilation, something like *that* would be a parlor trick to him. Right now, you need to focus. BBC is coming today to see the ballroom where the wedding will be held. It's *your* job to make sure charming and adorable Vincenza is here to meet them."

When she backed off yet again, I opened my eyes to meet her mahogany stare. "Whether it was Jer or not, anyone delivering that kind of message proves we're getting under Dorian's skin. The more irritated he is, the more likely he is to get sloppy and reveal himself."

"*Merp!*" Batdog yipped in agreement. Readjusting his position in my lap, he draped his head over my knee.

Lips sinking into a frown of disapproval, Mics peered down the bridge of her nose at him. "I'm so glad we worked this long to perfect your style, just so you can cover it in little black dog hairs."

Feigning innocence, I offered her a toothy grin. "Me too! I think it makes me more relatable."

Rummaging through the plethora of cosmetics Ego fetched for us—and no, the irony of *that* wasn't lost on me—Micah selected a rose-gold lip gloss. "Don't joke. Relatable is exactly what we need. You need to be the Vampire Queen of the people. All of the ladies should want to be you, while the guys want to be bitten by you."

"But no pressure," I huffed a humorless laugh, scratching Batdog's round little belly. "We should come up with some sort of plan or incantation to counter Dorian's magic if he tries anything like at the television studio again. I say that like it's something we can do. I mean, do we even have a spell guy? I feel we should. That seems like a more crucial thing to acquire than the right shade of eyeliner."

"Vinx! *Vincenza!*" Footfalls thundered through my bedroom. Hand on the door jam, Finn swung himself around the corner into the bathroom. "There you are! I think I found something. Like *really* found something!"

Pulling back, I blocked my nose with the back of my hand. "Whoa, dude. What the hell is that smell? Is that you?"

Micah seconded that question with a dry heave.

Unable to match Finn's speed, Carter jogged in behind him. Doubling over, he planted his hands on his knees in his struggle to catch his breath. "I've got to get my hands on more of that wine,"

Carter gasped. "That smell would be Finn, by the way. He's been glued to the computer in search of Jeremy and Rau. Gave up sleeping, and showering. *Good God, I'm out of shape. Whoa*! Anywho, the only thing he's eaten in days has been the blood delivered to him by the kitchen. Which as of late has belonged to a striped polecat—the smelliest animal on the planet. I arranged it as a joke. But, now he smells like dog shit baking in the sun, and I regret everything."

Eyes watering at his stench, I inched closer to the glassed-in shower enclosure. "Finn, how about if you stay right where you are, and tell me what you found?"

"It's not that bad," Finn *tsk*ed, then noticed his rumpled clothing. "Although, this *is* the same thing I was wearing when we got here. But, we're getting off topic." Snatching his phone from his back pocket, he tapped the screen then held it up for me to see. On it was a satellite map of Connecticut. "Rau is off the grid. They only bring him out for *big* spectacles. My guess? Since the police still have a warrant out for his arrest, and the last thing Markus wants is for Rau to get arrested. That happens, and he loses his favorite toy. But Jeremy? That kid is *everywhere*, and … they gave him a phone. One I have been able to ping numerous times to get a read on where they're keeping him. "

"Where is he?" Stare locked on that screen, as if it held the answer to the greatest mysteries of the world, I lowered Batdog to the floor.

With two fingers, Finn zoomed in to pull up an address on Town Walk Drive. "A condo near Yale University owned by … wait for it … Representative Alfonzo Markus. It seems Markus has taken it upon himself to keep tabs on your brother. No doubt wherever Markus is, his yes-man, Rutherford, is sure to follow."

"How can we use this?" Trying to pull himself to standing, Carter winced at what I guessed to be a runner's cramp, and hunched to the side.

Micah tapped a blush brush against her palm, chewing on her lower lip. "It means where we find one, we find the others. Play it right, and we could free Jeremy *and* take out Markus. That, sounds like a pretty damn good day."

Thumbing the home button, Finn stowed the phone back in his pocket. "Big flaw in that plan. We've made Vinx—the future Mrs. Dracula—the most recognizable woman on the planet. How could we sneak back into the states without paparazzi basically announcing to Markus that we're coming?"

Leaning my hip against the counter, my gaze traveled to all the paraphernalia strewn across it meant to turn me into a modern-day princess. "Why do we have to go to them? He's my brother. I'm getting married. I say we send him an invitation."

The tip of Micah's tongue toyed with the gold hoop in her lip. "It reeks of a trap, and not in a subtle way. Why would they subject themselves to that?"

"Maybe … if the potential gain was too good to resist? All those vampires in one place, with the entire world watching …" I trailed off, hoping one among them would pick up what I was laying down. "For that, Finn—conniving prick that he was—could be counted on. They would have a hell of a stage if they were able to sneak some of their sulfur serum overseas."

"Are you both *insane?*" Carter boomed, forcing himself upright. "You can't *possibly* be thinking about somehow *allowing* them to bring that shit here! What if they find a way to actually use it? What we've been working for would be completely destroyed. There's no coming back from televised genocide! No one will care about our screams of *drugged vampires* if they're set against a George R.R. Martin-style wedding massacre!"

"Then, I guess we better make damned sure they don't use it," I lobbed back. "The lure to turn this whole wedding on its ass will be impossible for them to resist. From there, we would need to use whatever connections we have to make *sure* they can smuggle the vials through. Once they step foot inside Castle Dracul, we seize control of their shipment and free my brother. Then, we take the serum public to substantiate our claims. It's risky, but we have the resources to pull it off."

My tirade was met by silence, smirks, and shifting glances.

"What?" Shoulders sagging, I prepared myself for their grocery list of reasons why my plan was ludicrous.

Finn dragged his palm over his chin, clucking his tongue against the roof of his mouth. "This is the first time you really *sounded* like a queen. One we will *gladly* follow."

"It's amazing what hours of prep and Micah's endless hounding can do," I scoffed, belittling the compliment. "I have to ask, why are you doing this, Finn? The endless research and tireless resolve, what's in this for you?"

Throwing his arms out wide, he brought his hands together in a sharp clap. "What could I *possibly* say that wouldn't sound contrite?"

Biting back every snarky sentiment I longed to spew, I dipped my head in invitation for him to speak his mind. "How about if you start with the truth?"

"I'm haunted by a past I can't fix." He managed, swallowing hard. "I've given up on you forgiving me, Vincenza. I'm sorry, but I have. I can't undo what I did, and—for *any* two people—there's just no getting passed that. What I need now, is to find a way to forgive *myself.*"

So many sentiments floated in the air between us. Those of compassion, regret, and clemency. Jutting out my chin, I voiced the words of hope that had been scrawled on my heart since the moment I learned Jeremy was alive. "Nothing can repair the mistakes of the past. But, we might just make a better future … for us all."

TWENTY-FOUR

VINX

Striding down the hall with my entourage, the heels of our shoes clacked over the marble floor, announcing our arrival to the milling camera crew and lighting technicians.

"Should we ask Vlad about this *before* adding the psycho holding his son hostage to the guest list?" Mics asked, hugging her wedding prep clipboard to her chest.

"There's no time." Forcing a smile, I waved to the reporter getting his face powdered in preparation for our interview. "The invitations are going out tomorrow. On this tight of a deadline, only those that *really* want to attend will be here."

"Are you kidding me?" Shoving his rolled sleeves farther up his forearms, Carter's tone dripped with bitterness. "It's the wedding of a living god. You could hold a ticket lottery at the door, and every biggot around the world would step on their own mother's face to get here."

That was it.

The first moment I got a shiver of anxious apprehension.

I agreed to marry Vlad as a powerplay to benefit our cause.

Not once did I hesitate, or give serious thought to what it was I was committing myself to. I would utter vows, and slide a ring onto the finger of Vlad Draculesti, binding myself to him the remainder of my days. In the eyes of the world, I would be his queen. Whatever I feel for *anyone* else would no longer matter.

For reasons I couldn't explain, my mind traveled to our hunt in the woods. The moonlight glistening over his features, while his fangs lengthened in trembling anticipation. Wind whipped his shirt back to reveal rock-hard muscle hidden beneath the fabric. His husky growl urged me on, "*Take her now.*"

As if cued by my thoughts, Vlad picked that moment to step out of his study clasping his cufflinks into place. Scanning the room, his stare sought me out. The saucy smile he tossed my way making me feel he could see every sensual thought playing through my mind.

With a hot rush of embarrassment creeping up my neck, I quickly averted my gaze to the floor, tripping over my own foot in the process.

"Vinx? You alright?" Carter's hand shot out to catch me. The warmth of his hand sizzled against my skin, my gums aching at the sirens of his blood.

Swallowing hard, I kept my lips pressed firmly together until the wave of desire could pass. "Vampires can't read minds, right? Not ever like, really old ones?" Before Carter could manage what was sure to be a befuddled answer, I steadied myself on my feet. "Never mind. He's coming over. Be cool. That last part was directed at me, not you."

"So, you're good then?" Face blank of any trace of emotion, Carter reiterated his original question.

Swatting away the overeager magi swarming to tend to his every need, Vlad's path led him straight to me. The suit he wore hugged his physique in tailored perfection, its charcoal shade brightening his sandstone hair to the molten glow of daybreak.

Catching my hand, he brought it to his lips to press a gentle kiss between my knuckles. "You look lovely, *copil*. Yet, I saw you falter. Is everything okay? Are you ill?"

"I'm fine, just suffering the side-effects of shoes a size too big, and opportunity leaping at the chance to embarrass me," I lied, hooking my hand through Vlad's offered elbow. Before he could escort me off to our press spot, I tilted my chin in Micah's direction. "The invitations need to go out today. I need you to see to that personally. Oh, and either force Finn to take a shower, or spray him with a hose. The plants are wilting as he walks by."

Turning on her heel with a crisp nod, she pinched Finn's shirt sleeve between her thumb and forefinger, and dragged him off with her.

As I squared my shoulders for the task ahead, I glanced down the expansive hall. Gold framed antique mirrors hung between marble pillars, adding an infinite feel to the sprawling space.

Shaking off a shiver of unease, my gaze tugged back to Carter. "Stay close," I whispered.

Chest puffed with purpose, he paid no attention to the man of myth beside me, but fell into stride at my heels. The interview started in the same fashion as the last, with Vlad and I making moon eyes at each other and answering questions about our whirlwind romance as well as the grand estate.

"Few people have ever been fortunate enough to step inside Castle Dracul," camera-ready smile plastered in place, the pretty boy reporter spoke directly into the camera instead of to us. "Yet in a week's time, the doors will be flung open to allow world leaders, celebrities, and the privileged elite to walk down this very hall. They will be ushered to the grand ballroom, where the world will watch as you recite your vows. Can you give us a hint of what we can expect that beautiful day?"

"*Other* than the angelic vision of my bride walking down the aisle?" Placing his hand on my lower back, Vlad gently pulled me to him.

Caught off guard by the natural familiarity of his embrace, my mask faltered for a beat. I was blinking up at Vlad in curious fascination when a face appeared in the mirror behind him.

Not just any face.

My face.

A fact I wouldn't have found odd … *if* the reflection mirrored my pose.

Standing alone, centered within the frame, daggers from her icy stare sliced into me. Her mouth moved, a haunting rasp tumbling from her lips. "*Spirit Lords, connect my ethereal cord with that of Vinx. Let us converge like the moon's light and darkness.*"

Swiveling in front of us, the reporter walked backwards, guiding us toward the grand reveal of the ballroom. "There are rumors that the flowers featured in the ceremony will be locally grown, and match the color scheme of the family crest of House of Draculesti. Can you confirm *either* of these top-secret details?"

Oblivious to anything but the threatening presence within the glass, I dragged my feet forward, wincing as the next mirror picked up where the previous left off. "*May we be one and the same in thought and in spirit.*"

"The flowers are all Vincenza's vision." Glancing my way, Vlad's brow creased with concern. "Vinx?"

Head whipping from one mirror to the next, that macabre vision met me at each surface. "*May my mind and will become one with hers.*"

My fingers tightened around Vlad's hand, clinging to him as the lifeline saving me from spiraling into the depths of madness. "Can you … see her?"

Glower set at full intensity, Vlad snapped his head in one direction then the other in search of a potential threat. "See who, *copil?* There's no one here but us and the crew."

Making a slicing motion with his hand in front of his throat, the reporter signaled for the cameraman to cut. "Is she okay? She's really pale. More so than usual, I mean."

Dropping Vlad's hand, I turned in a slow circle. That sinister version of me met me at every mirror, the voice from each rising up in ominous chorus. "*When I walk, she will walk with me. When I speak, she will echo each syllable. When I feel sorrow or lust, her heart will respond in kind.*"

Moving in a blur of speed, I gripped the edge of the nearest frame and hurled it off the wall. It crashed to the ground in a spray of shards, only for my reflection to appear within each sliver. Resonating from the shattered glass, the haunting visions added their voices to the malevolent choir. "*Thank you, Dark Lords, for your aid. May you make the cord between myself and Vincenza strong like the chains … of a prisoner.*"

Raking my fingernails down my cheeks, a shriek of terror ripped from my lungs.

My knees buckled, crumbling me to the floor where I was oblivious to the glass slicing into me.

"Vinx, what's wrong?"

"Vincenza, is someone harming you?"

"We could reschedule if she's sick."

The mirrors chanting tapered down into one spine-chilling message. "*Kill them, Vincenza. Kill them all.*"

Their words licked through my mind, awakening a red haze of bloodlust. Control slipping, my fangs ached to stretch from my gums.

Swirling his finger in a circular motion, the reporter signaled his crew to wrap things up. "This is clearly not the ideal time. We can reschedule when Miss Larow is feeling—"

"*Don't move.*" What was meant as a warning spewed forth in a threatening growl.

Polite façade crumbling, pretty boy reporter flushed with unease. "You know what? I didn't even *want* to do this bullshit vampire story! My producer *insisted* the ratings would be killer. But no one has *ever* won a Pulitzer for this kind of fluff piece. We're gathering our equipment, and we're getting out of here."

"*Kill them, Vincenza. Kill them all.*"

As the reporter flipped his helmet hair and started for the door, I caught sight of the vein trailing down the side of his neck, drumming with the hypnotic pulse of life. I dropped fang without realizing it, my pupils dilated by desire.

Rising into a low crouch, my lips curled from my teeth in a menacing snarl.

Carter's hand shot out. Seizing the reporter's forearm, he yanked him back. "Stay still."

"Vincenza! Stand down!" Curling his lip to flash his teeth, Vlad planted himself in my path. By all logical explanation his dominance in the bloodline *should* have subdued me. Unfortunately, we were well beyond the realms of logic.

Kill, Vincenza. Kill them all. Kill, Vincenza. Kill them all."

Ignoring Vlad's command, I snapped my jaws in response.

"Get your hands off of me!" The reporter ripped his arm out of Carter's hold, slapping his hand away. "I won't be a part of this twisted freak show!"

"I'm trying to save your life, you stupid bastard." Carter grumbled, positioning his body between the snooty reporter and me.

Inwardly, I screamed for my legs to stop.

I begged for my fangs to retract.

I prayed I wouldn't hurt anyone.

But, with crimson tears streaking my cheeks ... I lunged.

Left with no other option, Carter shoved the reporter aside and threw himself at me. There was no trace of fear in his eyes, only steadfast resolve.

Wrapping my arm around his neck, I weaved my fingers into his hair and wrenched his head to the side. I drove my fangs down hard and fast, the metallic tang of blood exploding in my mouth. It coursed out in a gushing stream thanks to Carter's hammering heart. Drinking deep with noisy slurps, I rode his body to the ground.

Hands hooked under my armpits, Vlad wrenched me off my fading prey. "Vincenza, enough!"

Still, my jaws stayed locked on Carter's throat, lifting his upper body off the ground with the power of my bite. Muscles locked rigid, his body twitched. I could feel the life leaking out of him, but could do nothing to break my hold.

"*Kill, Vincenza. Kill them all. Kill, Vincenza. Kill them all.*"

I felt his final breath breeze over my cheek, and something within me … broke.

Deafening silence rang through the hall.

The chanting stopped.

All motion stilled.

The fog controlling me rescinded, leaving me alone in the horror of my creation.

Finally able to release him, I dropped Carter as if afraid my touch could harm him further.

Peering up at Vlad, my stare pleaded for him to somehow erase my sin. "Wha … what happened? What have I done?"

Sorrow stealing over his features, he folded my trembling body into the comfort of his embrace. "The monster won the day, *copil*. For that, I am so very sorry."

TWENTY-FIVE

VLAD

I woke in full surrender.

Seeing everything, yet feeling nothing.

Even my fangs ripping from my gumline for the first time failed to register in my numb, submissive state. The physical pain of my body being mutilated by the change couldn't compare to the emotional anguish of knowing I'd turned my back on my beliefs, and damned my soul. To endure that torment, my only choice was to deaden myself to it.

If anyone or anything stood between me and my return to Jusztina, I took them out with reckless abandon. A cloud of death storming through the night.

History remembers me as a merciless killer. That journey home was when I earned such a title. Those whose larnax I didn't tear out with my teeth, met death by the sword. My legacy is as the Impaler.

What the books don't mention is that it's a deed not easily perfected. Embed the blade too far forward and the weight of the body causes them to split right down the middle, spilling their entrails into the grass. Too far back, and the sword can't hold their weight, causing their forms to slump to the ground. By the time I arrived back in Transylvania, my vicious artistry planted a forest of dangling corpses in my wake.

Being the coward that he was, Murad saw his soldiers losing ground outside of the city, he rallied what was left of his men and ordered an immediate retreat. Not wanting to fight someone else's war alone, the Saxon's scrambled to follow.

Dismounting from the back of Garreg, my blood splattered boots sank into Transylvania soil. The courtyard was eerily quiet, cautious eyes of frightened residents peeking out through closed shutters. One glimpse of me, and they ducked from sight. Not that I could blame them. The fact that I damned myself for them made me no less of a monster. Lifting my chin toward the castle I called home, I sniffed the air and felt a shiver of … something. Jusztina was here. I could smell her … and the heady waves of fear radiating off of her.

"Vlad?" A soft voice ventured.

Head snapping around, my upper lip quivered into a growl.

Elena, Jusztina's handmaiden, recoiled at the sight of me. Fright widened her eyes at the filthy slick of soot, grim, and gore covering me.

"What is it?" I snapped, heavy drops of blood dripping from my hair.

Wringing her hands, Elena's voice cracked with trepidation. The delicious aroma of her terror made my mouth fill with saliva. "I … *we*— meaning my family and I—tried to keep Jusztina hidden. A man found her. He sought her out specifically, went door to door ransacking homes in search of her."

Tipping my head, I sniffed the air a second time.

"*Dorian*," his name rumbled from my chest in a thunderous boom of hate.

"There's more." Elena risked a step forward, her hand shooting out to halt my charge. "She had the baby, Vlad. You have a son. He is up there, with both of them."

Driven by wrath, my form exploded into a wall of fog. Swooping and spiraling, I rode the wind, climbing the face of the castle's tallest tower. I entered through the balcony of the bed chamber Jusztina and I shared, solidifying next to the bed.

"Jusztina?" I breathed her name into the darkness.

"What a beautifully theatrical entrance," Dorian chuckled. He emerged from the shadows, gripping Jusztina's upper arm. Cradled in the crook of his elbow rested my bundled newborn son. Face morphing into a sneer, his eyes narrowed to dangerous slits. "You've done it. You've given yourself to The Dragon. I can feel the pulse of its influence radiating off of you. How … *enticing*."

"You can't imagine what this feels like, Dorian." Seeing an opportunity, I battled back my bubbling hatred and fought to maintain a steady, neutral tone. "The lure of raw power lying in wait for me to tap into. It's an endless realm of unfathomable possibilities. You say you have no need for it. I wonder if that's so." Holding up one hand, I turned it over in a pantomimed cursory inspection. "It's all you ever wanted, and now it's *mine*. Of course, we could discuss a trade. You let my family go, and I will give myself over to you. You can plot, scheme, and experiment on me all you like in order to draw The Dragon out, just as soon as they are safely released."

Tears slipped from Jusztina's lashes, zigzagging over her ruddy cheeks. "Vlad, please don't let him hurt the baby."

"Hush, *floare*," I softly soothed, my stare locked on the man who literally held my heart in his hands. "Dorian and I can handle this like gentlemen."

"You drank of the sacrament and pledged yourself to the beast," Dorian deliberated, dragging his tongue over his top teeth. "You belong to it as long as you walk this earth. The only way to part you from *Drákon* now would be by his choosing."

I pulled my sword from its sheath, and tossed it aside. It landed on the wood floor with a sharp clang. "I make this my vow: allow my wife and child to leave, and I will let you run whatever trials you deem necessary until you've claimed what you seek."

Sucking air through his teeth, Dorian tilted his head. "Ah, Vlad, you always have been all brawn and no brain. You are right about one thing, I do still long for The Dragon. However, as I said, the choice to be expelled from you now lies with *Drákon*. I do think I could sway his interest," a vindictive smile coiled at the corners of his mouth, deadly as a pit of vipers, "... with the right sacrifice."

My fangs lengthened from my gums, earning a frightened gasp from my trembling bride. "Hear me, Dorian Gray. *You will* not *harm either of them.*"

The baby beginning to fuss, Dorian clucked quietly and bounced him. *Him.* This malicious man comforted *my son*, whose face I had yet to see. "Oh, *I* have no intention of hurting anyone." Peering up from under his brow, he offered me a mask of faux innocence. "Ultimately, that decision lies with *you*."

"Vlad, what's happening?" Stare locked on her crying newborn, Jusztina's voice cracked.

"Everything will be fine, my darling. Won't it, Dorian?" The words were slathered in threat. Bending my knees, I sank into a low crouch. "We're not going to play games with lives of the innocent."

Dorian stepped back toward the edge of the balcony in wide strides, dragging my family along with him. "Oh, but the games are just beginning. I would draw in those shiny new teeth of yours, Vlad. Especially considering I am currently in control of *all* you hold dear."

"*Vlad?*" Jusztina pleaded, stumbling back at Dorian's insistence.

Biting my tongue hard enough to taste a metallic hint of blood, I forced my fangs to retract. "How does this end, Dorian? You tell me."

Throwing his head back, his bawdy guffaw echoed through the valley below. "It ends, my old friend, with a choice." Laughter dying on his lips, his vicious glare snapped in my direction. "You can save *one*. The other will be sacrificed in the name of *Drákon*." With a shift of his upper body, he dangled the baby closer to the precipice, then Jusztina. "Who will you spare? Your bride? Or, your baby?"

"I'm not going to choose." Knowing my strength and speed were now heightened, I scanned the space between us, calibrating the proper route of attack to ensure the safety of my family.

Eyebrows raised, Dorian challenged me with another bold step toward that drop-off into oblivion. "My game, my rules. Pick, Vlad. Elsewise, I march all three of us right over the rail. I'll walk away from the plummet. How do you think they'll fair?"

Jusztina's red-rimmed stare lobbed from Dorian to me. "Vlad, you must keep the baby safe. *Promise me*!"

"It seems the lady has made her selection," Dorian *tsk*ed. Yanking on her wrist, he tugged Jusztina back until the rail pressed against her hip. "Will you honor her request, I wonder? I mean, if you save *her* you two could *always* make another child. That is, if she ever forgives you for allowing your son to die."

"No!" Fighting to free herself, Jusztina struggled against his hold. "Vlad, you mustn't let any harm come to our boy!"

Moving in a licking tendril of fog, I scooped my sword off the floor and held it at the ready before me. "Dorian, *enough*! You want me? I'm right here! Let them go and fight me like a man, you despicable coward!"

Dorian's head cocked as if genuinely perplexed. "Haven't you figured it out yet? I don't want to fight you. Knowing of the evil that roosts inside you, I want to see what happens when it's unleashed on the world. You see, you once stole everything from me. The power that was to be mine, and the glorious reign that would have followed. Now, I plan to return that favor. The stalling ends now. Make your choice, or I shall make it for you."

All of the power The Dragon bestowed on me, and I stood crippled by indecision. Could I take Dorian out before he forced either over the edge? Unsure of my new strength and abilities, that was an unsolvable riddle. Not when it meant life or death for one I held dear.

Teetering the baby over the cut-stone ledge of the balcony, gleeful lunacy flashed in the depths of Dorian's gaze. "Time's up. Who shall it be?"

"*No!*" Shrieks tearing from her lungs, Jusztina threw her weight into Dorian's shoulder. His body twisted in the opposite direction, pivoting the baby away from harm. Unable to pull back from the momentum of her strike, Jusztina hurdled over the bannister. Falling from view, the fabric of her gown snapped in the wind behind her.

"*Jusztina!*" Not knowing if I could survive such a fall, I had no choice but to leave the baby behind as I hurled over the rail. Throwing myself into a steep swan dive, the world zipped past in a whistling blur.

Even with her raven hair lashing her cheeks a brilliant pink, a peaceful stillness stole over Jusztina's features. One delicate hand reached for me. Not out of desperation for a savior, but in the sweet sentiment of goodbye to all that should have been. Frantically clawing at the air, I tried in desperation to close the gap of space between us.

Our fingertips touched ... at the same instant her body slammed into the cobblestone ground. While I landed in an easy crouch, the impact rippled through Jusztina in a gruesome crackle of breaking bones. Her porcelain skin drained ashen, a pool of blood stretching around her.

"Vlad?" She managed in a weak croak, her breathing a labored medley of rattling wheezes.

Taking a knee at her side, I brushed the hair from her face. Even that tender touch elicited a pained wince from my crumbled angel. "Yes *floare*. I'm here."

"I ... named our son Mihnea Rau." Lids growing heavy by the pull of eternal sleep, Jusztina's lashes fluttered against the apples of her cheeks. "Take ... care of each ... other."

One final breath whispered over her bluing lips, and she stilled.

My love.

My life.

My purpose.

Gone.

Delicately lifting her from the ground, I folded her into my arms and showered her with blood-tinged tears. How long I sat there, rocking my broken beauty, I couldn't say. Lost in the nightmare of a world without her, the sound of a door creaking open drew me back to the horrifying here and now. Elena and her family emerged from their modest cabin within the square. Each held a bushel of wildflowers cradled in their arms.

Easing Jusztina to the ground, I stood as they neared, fully expecting them to cast me out for the demon I had become. To my surprise, I found no trace of accusation etched on their faces, only genuine compassion.

"The men who descended upon this village were not kind," Elena's tear-filled gaze fixed on her fallen lady, her chin quivering. "They claimed whatever they desired with brutal force."

Standing at Elena's elbow, the lass I guessed to be her younger sister cast her stare to the ground, a plum-colored bruise shading her jawline.

Their father cleared his throat, his narrow chest puffed with purpose. "We watched you single-handedly drive their armies into retreat. T'was like nothing I've ever seen. I don't know what you are, lad." Before my lips could part to attempt an explanation, he held up one arthritic hand to halt me. "Mind you, I'm not asking. As far as me and my kin are concerned, you're an avenging angel sent to protect us. You must be. We only wish your kindness didn't come at such a steep price."

Freefalling tears traced paths of sorrow down Elena's face, dripping from her chin. "Your wife was a kind, caring spirit. Please, m'lord, may we honor her in a fitting fashion?"

Dumbfounded, the closest I could come to a response was stumbling back with a brief nod. Crouching down alongside Jusztina, Elena laid the armful of flowers next to her face. Her sisters and father mirrored the act, spreading the arch of colorful blooms over my bride's head in a halo of beauty befitting her life and spirit. Their mother shuffled forward to set a flickering candle next to Jusztina's shoulder. Doors throughout the courtyard opened, spilling more townsfolks into the square. One by one, they added their offerings of love to the vigil. A wreath of adoration stretched around my selfless wife, stolen from the Earth far too soon.

"Get the hell out of here, you traitorous snake!" Hearing our somber moment interrupted by such a gruff command, I swiveled to find Renfield—Commander of the Transylvania Guard—rooting himself in a wide stance to block Dorian's path.

"Call off your dog, Vlad, or, I won't hand over your consolation prize." Ignoring Renfield completely, Dorian lifted his arms to remind me of the precious cargo he was still in possession of.

"Let him by." Hands curling into fists at my sides, I stalked straight for Dorian. While grief momentarily distracted me from my newborn *copil*, ensuring his safety became paramount. "Give me the boy, or I swear to you I—"

"Calm yourself," Dorian interrupted, unceremoniously dropping the baby into my arms. "No need for pointless threats. I have no use for your smelly, squirming larva. At least … not today. Even so, this kindness comes with a warning. Your loss today bought you time, *only*. One day, when you think I've long since forgotten, I will take great pleasure in ripping apart what remains of your family. Perhaps then you will unleash the full power of The Dragon on the world. Hold him tight, papa. Your days together are numbered."

A gust of wind swelled, and Dorian vanished.

TWENTY-SIX

VINX

E yes snapping open, I bolted upright. Odd flecks of emerald danced through the room, causing me to blink hard to focus. Glancing up, I found the source was a stained-glass window designed in the shape of a willow tree.

"This … isn't my room," I muttered to the walls.

"I brought you back to my bed chamber to watch over you." Vlad's frame filled the adjacent bathroom doorway, a glass of water cradled between his palms. "I felt it was best after all that transpired."

Clarity snapped back with an electrifying jolt. Curling my legs under me, I sprang to my knees, ready to dart for the door. "Carter! Is he okay?"

Vlad crossed the room on silent steps, and set the water on the mahogany bedside table. "Your friend is with the Court. We will know more soon."

"Know more? So, he's ... not dead?" I dared to hope.

In place of an answer, Vlad's face folded with compassion.

An inhumane sob choked from my throat. "I did it. I killed him."

"He had vampire blood in his system," Vlad explained, rubbing his hands together to dry the perspiration from the glass. "They are watching, and waiting for him to wake."

Dragging my fingers through my hair, my feeble mind raced to keep up. "That's not possible. He's a recovering addict. He wouldn't voluntarily feed off of someone. I can't believe after living with two vampires and managing to avoid temptation, he would slip up with some rando."

"He fed from no one, of that I am certain." Picking back up the glass of water I had yet to touch, Vlad placed it directly in my hands. "He drank of the magi wine. It's laced with—"

"Vampire blood," I finished for him, recalling Carter's explosive reaction after treating himself to the bottle in his room. "But, this is a good thing, right? He died with Nosferatu blood in his system. He'll wake up a newborn vamp I owe a *huge* apology to."

Vlad waited to speak until I dutifully took a sip of water. "Many years ago, rules were put into place for all those that lived and served at Castle Dracul. When a potential—which you know as the magi—died in service of a royal, it was left up to the Court to decide if they were worthy to take a seat amongst their ranks as an Elder. Carter served you, the future queen. The Court is deliberating now on if he will be allowed to rise again."

"And if they vote against it?" Dreading the answer, I gripped the midnight blue bedding in white knuckled fists.

"A silver stake will be driven through his heart."

"Of, *fucking*, course it will." Chin dropping to my chest, I ground the heels of my palms into my eyes. "What about the reporter and the camera crew?"

"All were influenced. As far as they know, it was a lovely interview. Unfortunately, the X-ray machine at the airport *mysteriously* wiped away all of their footage. They have already called to schedule a phone interview in attempts to salvage their story."

Gnawing on my lower lip, I shook my head. "How the hell did we get here? I never meant to hurt anyone."

Vlad plunged his hands into the pockets of his slacks, and began pacing at the foot of the bed. "I ... must tell you something you will likely find upsetting."

"More so than me killing one of my best friends?" Eyebrows hitched in disbelief, my shoulders sagged. "Now I get why people feared you. *That* is straight up terrifying."

"Your actions were incredibly out of character. I worried you would harm others, or yourself." Reaching into the breast pocket of his button-down shirt, Vlad extracted a brushed-copper ice pick with a dangerously sharp point. "While you slept—"

Lips pursed, I bobbed my head to signal I caught up. "You drank my blood to learn the truth. Well, thanks for not biting me without consent. That would have been *really* intrusive. I mean, by etiquette standards, a quick stabbing is far more chivalrous."

"I apologize for taking such liberties." Rolling the ice pick over the back of his knuckles, Vlad flipped it point down and tucked it safely away. "However, when you hear what I've learned, you will see a far more egregious offense has been committed."

Talons of dread tightened around my throat. "We're up to murder and assault. Too many more big reveals and I'm going to need a fake passport and a new identity."

Taking a seat beside me, Vlad rested his elbows on his knees. Chin tipped in my direction, he swallowed hard before speaking. "Somewhere in the midst of your journey, Dorian Gray bewitched you."

Unsure of how to respond, I brought the glass to my lips and gulped down the remainder of its contents. I wanted to argue that it couldn't be true, that I never met the guy. How, then, could I explain recognizing his voice at the studio? Or, how its silky cadence paralyzed me. "How ... is that possible?"

"I told you of his dark magic. You met him once, where he coerced you to drink of his blood as part of a binding spell. He forced you to do his bidding, and erased your memories when he was through."

Tangible hatred brewed in the depths of Vlad's stare, bubbling like a cauldron of poison.

Hands shaking, I set the empty glass aside. "What did he make me do?"

"It wasn't you."

Lacing my fingers in hopes of steadying them, I dropped them in my lap. "It can't be worse than what I'm imagining. Just tell me."

Bed squeaking under his weight, Vlad shifted to face me. "He made you kill for him, Vincenza."

"Who?"

"I could pick up very little about him, only the zing of magic in his blood after you fed. From what I could tell, he was a necromancer."

"Jeremy." Uttering my brother's name drove the dagger of guilt deeper into my gut. "I must've killed the man who brought him back."

Stare traveling over my face, Vlad's expression was a portrait of empathy. "Through your exchange of blood, Dorian can draw you under his thrall whenever he chooses. That is what transpired today. You mustn't blame yourself."

"He warned us to stop the media spots. We didn't listen, and it cost Carter his life." Feeling myself spiraling into a pit of self-loathing, I sniffed back my misery and squared my shoulders. "I want him out of my head. How do we break his thrall?"

Vlad caught one of my trembling hands, and held it tenderly in his, his thumb tracing small circles on the inside of my wrist. "The bond was formed in blood, and must be broken the same way."

The scars on my neck throbbed at the harsh recollection of his bite. "What now?"

A crooked smile tugged at the perfect bow of his lips. Unbuttoning his right cuff, Vlad rolled his sleeve up to his elbow. "I have already tasted you, *copil*. For this to work, it must be your turn. If, you'll have me?"

"*Copil*. You keep calling me that. What does it mean?" Even as I formed the question, my gaze locked on his arm. Drawn there by the alluring pull of his blood.

156

Freehand sinking into the mattress, he scoot closer. With silken strands of russet hair falling across his forehead, he peered at me from under his brow. "It means *baby,* as that is what you are. The beautiful baby vampire who will be queen."

"I like that," I managed in a throaty whisper, a shiver of longing dancing through my core.

Leaning in, his lower lip teased over mine, tempting me with the promise of his touch. "As my queen, I will give myself to you whenever you crave. Will you have me?"

My lips parted in a sigh. "Yes … I'll have you."

Enveloping me in his embrace, Vlad pulled me to him with my back pressed to his chest. His fangs lengthened, the smooth curve of one brushing my cheek. Crossing his arm over my chest, he bit down on his wrist. Ruby pearls swelled from his flesh in offering to me.

I dragged my tongue over the wounds, which earned an appreciative moan that rumbled from Vlad's tightly clenched lips. Spurred on by his audible desire, I wrapped my mouth around his wrist, and sucked deep. The bouquet of his flavor exploded in my mouth, tasting of lust, strength, and undeniable power.

Lost in a blood-drunk haze, my senses heightened. Every sound was an angelic chorus. Every touch orgasmic bliss. Somewhere in the midst of euphoric rush, the thread binding me to Dorian snapped. In its place, cords of fate, trust, and acceptance braided together in a thick rope connecting Vlad's life with mine. A rope I knew could easily be twisted into a noose.

Not that I cared.

Or could manage a thought outside of *him.*

Turning to face the Lord of Darkness, I settled onto his lap with my knees tucked on either side of him.

"Are all women in this time so bold?" he murmured, hands weaving into my hair.

"Only those that know what they want." Hips rocking against him, my lips claimed his with feverish intent.

Grabbing my waist, he flipped me onto the mattress, pinning me beneath his weight. The points of his fangs dragged over my exposed throat. "Is there something you desire, my queen?"

Upper body lifting off the mattress, I sought his mouth once more. "If you have to ask, I'm being too subtle."

With a low, throaty chuckle, his fangs retracted. "There will be plenty of time for that, *copil*. An eternity in fact ... *after* we are wed."

Propped up on my elbows, I blinked his way in disbelief. "Seriously? You're going to kiss me like that and walk away? That borders on cruel and unusual punishment."

Dotting a kiss to my shoulder, Vlad tilted his face to mine and gifted me a mischievous grin. "I do, indeed. I have been with but one other woman, my late wife Jusztina. The next I lie with will be my bride, as well."

Lips screwed to the side, my disappointed libido spoke for me. "You know, for the Lord of Darkness, you're kind of a prude."

Nipping at the fabric of my sweater, he gave it a playful tug with his teeth. "And, for a lab created vampire, you possess a raw, primal quality I've never seen before. It's intoxicating."

Rolling on to my side, I rested my head on my hand. "*One* other woman? *Really though*? How is that possible? I mean, do you know what countless women would do to you ... or for you?"

"I have some idea. Some sent sketches. They were equal parts impressive, and deeply disturbing." Bounding off the bed, his hands encircled my wrists and tugged me to my feet. "Soon, my queen, and then forever. For now, we need to see to your friend, and alert the Court that Dorian Gray no longer holds sway over you."

"This sudden need to leave wouldn't have *anything* to do with your own slipping resolve, now would it?" I teased, stepping in close enough for my chest to brush his.

"And she's clever, too!" Vlad gasped in mock surprise, and dotted a kiss to the tip of my nose.

TWENTY-SEVEN

VINX

Leaving the safe confines of his room, knives of guilt sliced slashes of self-loathing into me. Apprehension over Carter's well-being knotted my gut, while my body vibrated with the rush of Vlad's blood still singing through my veins. How was it possible to feel crushed and bullet-proof all at the same time?

Whether Vlad felt my anxiety through our blood-bond, or picked up on the waves of it radiating off of me, I couldn't say. Whatever the cause, he pulled up short. Linking his pinkie finger with mine, he gave a gentle tug. "If it comes to it, I will speak in his favor."

Kind as his sentiment was, it only made me feel worse. Why should I be shown that or *any* benevolence when Carter's life hung in the balance because of me?

Footfalls pounding down the hall spared me from forcing a response. Elodie rounded the corner at a full sprint, her arms and legs pumping like well-oiled pistons. Coming to an abrupt stop in front of Vlad, she clapped her fist over her heart and dipped her head in a brief bow of respect. "Lord Draculesti, Carter is awake. The Court requests your presence in their deliberations over what is to become of him."

Grasping Vlad's shirt sleeve in both hands, I glanced from him to Elodie and back again. "What does that mean? It doesn't sound good."

"It doesn't mean anything, yet." In a rare show of compassion, Elodie stepped closer and pried my hands free from the fistfuls of fabric. "With Vlad newly awakened, they wouldn't dare make such a decision without consulting him. If for no other reason than to set a precedent for how these matters should be addressed in the future. Your friends are in Carter's room with him. Whatever is to come, you need to be with them."

I stared down the hall like it was the long walk down the green mile. "They're going to hate me."

"Why would they hate you?" Spine rigid, Elodie tilted her head in schoolmarm challenge.

"Because ... I killed him."

"Odd, since I *just* said he's awake. If you killed him, you didn't do a very thorough job." I opened my mouth to argue, only to have Elodie close her eyes for a beat and shake her head. "You're thinking like a human. Stop it. Today, you sired Carter. That should be celebrated. Not mourned."

"And if the Court votes to stake him?" I countered.

"Then, you can hate *them*." Waving Vlad around me, Elodie pursed her lips and jerked her head toward Carter's looming door. "We have to go. You, wrestle your inner demons another minute or two, then get over your bullshit and go see your friends."

Vlad glanced back, clearly wanting to comfort me further. Planting one hand in the center of his back, Elodie thwarted his efforts by rushing him along.

Left alone in the hall, I toyed with the idea of running. Disappearing to some uninhabited island, where I could find a quaint little cave to dwell in and never have to worry about hurting another person, was a tempting prospect. But, if such a place *did* exist, the cell service was bound to be terrible.

Squashing that as a viable alternative, I swiveled on my heel and marched to Carter's door before I could talk myself out of it. Fist raised to knock, I hesitated. My heart constricted in a tight fist of fear.

Before I could reach a decision on whether to knock or bail, the six-panel door flew open.

"Vincenza! I *knew* I smelled you!" Micah gushed, grabbing me in a tight bear hug. "We've been so worried! Are you okay?"

Arms pinned to my sides by her exuberant embrace, I stood pencil straight. "Why were you worried about me? You saw Carter, you know what I did."

Keeping hold of my upper arms, Mics pulled back to look me in the face. "Like you're the only one that's ever lost control? Hell, at this point it's a requirement to be in our club."

Shrugging out of her hold, I ducked around her into the room. While Finn lounged in a wing-back chair in the corner, clicking away on his phone, there was no sign of Carter. "You weren't there. You didn't see it. I attacked him like a wild animal! If it wasn't for him *accidentally* having vampire blood in his system, he would be dead right now!"

Micah jabbed one hand on her hip in exasperation. "Did you bump your head on the way in here, and forget all that we've been through? I killed a stranger, *and* emotionally scarred a stripper."

Not bothering to look up from the screen, Finn raised his hand. "I ate your family."

"See?" Mics stabbed a hand in his direction. "We all have our shit, Vinx. You didn't turn your back on me when I messed up, and I would never do that to you. Plus, Carter is *alive*. Sure, he's going to have to adapt to some dietary changes, but he's *okay*."

"W—where is he?" Drifting to the bed, I ran my hand over the rumpled comforter.

"He's in the restroom, getting cleaned up." Eyes narrowing, Micah tilted her head. "What ... is up with your face?"

"Huh?" Fearing I had been caught with my hand in the proverbial cookie jar, I wiped my mouth on the back of my hand. "Nothing."

Of course, Finn picked that moment to chime in. Dropping his phone in his lap, he glanced up in cursory inspection. "No, she's right. Your complexion is all red and blotchy. I've seen that look before!" He pointed a finger of accusation my way. "*You got laid.*"

Those were the first words Carter heard when he emerged from the bathroom.

He was attractive *before* the change, gifted with laid-back style and charm.

Standing there now, he could only be described as heart-achingly beautiful. Hair a deep shade of decadent butterscotch. The lines of his face sculpted perfection. Skin flawless porcelain. Gone were his blood-soaked clothes, replaced by a pair of cotton pajama pants that sat low enough to reveal the deep V of his hip bones plunging downward.

Heat rushing up my neck, I scrambled to clarify Finn's claim. "No No, I didn't! I haven't had sex. Well, I mean I *have* had sex. Did it with him, in fact." Unnecessary head jerk in Finn's direction. "He does this little trick with his hand that I really enjoyed. Point is, I haven't had sex *today*, with him or anyone." Realizing words were still spewing from my lips, I dropped my chin to my chest and tried to cap off my ramble. "Just so everyone knows."

Finn's ebony eyebrows raised. "That ... was surreal."

Gulping down my bout of stupid, I peered Carter's way with a face full of questions. "Are you—"

Not waiting for my words to form, Carter latched on to me in a flash of vampiric speed. Gathering me in his arms, he squeezed tight. Cheek pressed to my hair, he breathed me in ... then recoiled with a jerk. What looked like accusation darkened his stare to a deep ocean blue. The tight knit of his brow reading as betrayal.

Heightened vampire senses. He could smell Vlad all over me.

I shouldn't have been embarrassed by that. I was days away from marrying the vampire lord. Even so, my mouth opened and shut in search of some paltry sentiment that could somehow wash his hurt away.

"Dorian Gray had me under some sort of magical thrall," I began, voice weak and wavering. "That's why I attacked you. The only way to break his hold, was through a blood bond."

Silence.

Arms sliding to his sides, Carter backed away.

Reaching for him, I reconsidered and let my hand drop. "Please, say something."

"He can't." Elodie strode in, positioning herself at the foot of the bed, she clasped her hands behind her back. The Court floated in behind her, forming a shoulder to shoulder line at the far side of the room. "As a potential member of the Court, it is required that he become of one mind and one voice with all of the elders. This is accomplished by mastering the art of telepathic communication. His first test, which he was charged with the instant he awoke, is to commit himself to a vow of silence until he can accomplish this sacred practice."

"Does that mean ...?"

Hint of a smile twitching at the corners of her lips, Elodie dipped her head in a nod of confirmation. "Carter Westerly gave his life in service to a soon-to-be royal. It is the verdict of the Court that—upon completion of his introductory trial—he be awarded a seat as an elder." With a crisp turn that made her heels click together, she faced the man of the hour. "If this is what you want, Carter, I ask that you take a knee."

Without a moment's pause, he followed her command.

"Whoa, now." Palms out, I pumped the brakes on whatever ceremonial ritual was about to play out. "I feel we are lacking some crucial details here. I mean, what happens if he can't accomplish this telepathic voodoo? Or, slips up and speaks? The guy should know what's going to happen if he accidentally stubs his toe and let's fly the customary expletive."

"This trial tests the commitment and resolve of each potential elder. If he cannot achieve it, or breaks his vow, his membership amongst our ranks will be terminated."

I rolled my head in a half-circle, a cue for her to finish what seemed to be an ominous threat. "Meaning?"

Drifting forward from the haunting line of black, Renfield drew back his hood with gnarled, bony hands. "If he cannot, he will be put to death."

"Wow." I winced. "No learning curve at all, huh?"

My gaze flicked to Carter, regretting every word that went unspoken between us.

Everything had changed.

What we were to each other.

What we could be.

The one thing I needed before diving into forever with Vlad, was the closure of a heartfelt conversation. Fate chose to deny me that.

As if he could read every qualm written on my face, Carter's stare locked on me while Elodie uttered the words that would bind him to his fresh destiny. "The salute in House Dracul is a fist clutched over our heart. For while the muscle beneath no longer beats, it does not hinder our love, duty, or honor. From this day forth, Carter Westerly, you shall give of yourself body and soul to protect the Nosferatu bloodline, and our noble king and queen. If this is your vow, secure your pledge with our customary salute."

Nostrils flaring with exuberant passion, Carter clapped his fist to his chest.

His solemn vow sworn, the other courtsmen swarmed. Encircling him, they laid hands on his shoulders and arms, and bowed their heads in silent prayer.

Shuffled aside by their huddle, I caught Elodie's elbow. "How long does it take? For them to master telepathy, I mean?"

Not wanting to miss a moment of the ceremony, Elodie rose on tiptoe to peer over the blockade of weaved cloaks. "That depends on him. Only when he has something truly worth saying will the gift come."

TWENTY-EIGHT
VLAD

For fifty-four years, I had been diligent.

Believing every word of Dorian's threats.

With stones of preparation, I constructed a fortress around all I cared about. That began with the formation of an army. Looking to my trusted guards and the brave townspeople of Transylvania, I gave them the choice to become like me. Renfield, ever loyal to his post, was the first. After witnessing his strength and agility once reborn, others lined up to join our ranks.

Calling ourselves the Nosferatu—taken from the Hungarian/Romanian word for creatures that drink blood—our numbers grew. While I remained selective about who I exchanged my essence with, my fanged children were not. Overcome by desire, they would lose themselves in their dark passions until death or conversion became the only option for their drained human mate. It didn't take long before our kind blanketed the earth … in a cloak of death and destruction.

Accepting my role as father to them all, I led by example, creating rules to guide us in peaceful union alongside humans. Those who chose not to obey, were brought before me. The punishments doled out firm and unforgiving. No leniency was granted when it came to innocent lives.

It didn't take long for me to realize that a world ladled with death and violence was no place for a growing boy. Combine that with the fact that by my side was the very *first* place Dorian would look for Rau, and the decision was made for me. Beseeching Father Van Helsing, the priest who married Jusztina and I, I sought refuge for my darling son. To my great relief, Van Helsing obliged and whisked Rau to the Neamt Monastery. I told no one where he was. Instead, I watched from afar, year after year, as my boy grew. His life was a precious pearl I would sacrifice anything to protect. Even so, accepting that never made our visits through the years any easier. Each time, Rau—now older than I would ever appear—begged me to turn him. That we may once again be together as a family. Seeing the depths of depravity exhibited by so many of my fanged offspring, I considered that a fate worse than death. One I could never inflict on him. Knowing my boy to have the same stubborn streak as his father, I issued a command to all Nosferatu. No one was to turn my son, death being the penalty to any who dare ignore this steadfast law.

For fifty-four years I remained vigilant, watching and waiting for Dorian to make his move. All the while watching The Dragon's seed seeping across the land in a toxic sludge of wickedness … because of *me*.

Seated on the throne Renfield *insisted* on having commissioned for me, I rubbed my palm over my forehead. The moon was not yet at it's highest, yet I had already seen to over a dozen offenses brought before me.

"I was chased through the streets by a torch and pitch fork wielding crowd!" Pleading his case, the young vampire—with stringy black hair and hooked-beak nose—gestured wildly. "What choice had I, *except* to defend myself?"

Hand dropping to the arm rest, my fingers dangled over its rounded edge. "You slaughtered an entire village," I stated, tone devoid of emotion.

"*To protect myself!*" Strands of hair stuck to the young vamp's neck, held there by the crusted blood of his kills.

"You killed the daughter of a duke, they were seeking rightful retribution." With a snap of my fingers, I gestured Renfield over, ready to make my ruling.

"They are sheep!" The accused hissed, daring to drop fang in my presence. "*We are wolves!* I will not cower to creatures that are beneath me! This world could be ours if we were led by one *brazen enough* to seize it."

A sharp ripple of air, and I was on him.

Knocked flat on his back, I crushed his throat beneath my boot. It wouldn't kill him, but it *did* provide a painful reminder that my power far exceeded his own. Rocking onto the ball of my foot I waited for the first *crunch* to tell me I had his complete attention. "Do you think this is an argument I haven't heard before? There is *always* some cocksure *copil* vampire ready to show their strength by painting the world with blood. I will tell you the same thing I told *all* struck by that exact delusion." Squatting down, I applied a bit more of my weight to his wind-pipe. "Humans outnumber us ten-thousand to *one*. If we don't abide by rules to coexist with them, they *will* turn on us. And, who could blame them? We're parasitic leeches suckling at the vein of civility."

"My Lord?" Clearing his throat, Renfield assumed a wide-legged stance with his hands clasped behind his back.

Pushing off my knees to stand, I retracted my foot. "Take him to the roof of the tallest tower. At dawn, he meets the sun."

Renfield beckoned to the two guards stationed on either side of the door with a snap of his fingers. Jumping to attention, they darted over to carry out my orders. Hooking the condemned under his arms, they dragged him out kicking and screaming.

Renfield patiently waited for his cries to fade before updating me on our roster. "That was the last, sire. Only four put to death. Perhaps word of what will be tolerated is finally beginning to spread."

"Or, they're getting better at covering it up." Flopping back down in my walnut throne, I let my head fall back against its intricate, hand-carved designs. "You look thin, old friend. Are you not feeding?"

Despite his sunken cheeks, Renfield's chest puffed with purpose. "I allow myself but one drop of blood per night, m'lord. To live as example to others that our kind *are* capable of restraint."

"A noble venture indeed." My head dipped in a bow of respect.

"Thank you, sire. I did want to discuss with you an idea I had to safeguard that you are surrounded by trustworthy advisors."

With two fingers I waved the conversation on. "Speak."

"The line of human supporters here in Transylvania that want to be turned is growing long. I propose we initiate them on a trial basis, making them prove themselves before they are turned. *Only* when they are found worthy would they earn a place within your inner circle, and join our family of Nosferatu here at Castle Dracul."

Drumming my fingers against the arm rest, I mulled over the suggestion. "It would require a human we can trust to oversee the potentials. One that seeks not to be turned themselves."

"*Father Van Helsing!*" Sprinting into the throne room, Marius— one of our newer charges—skidded to a stop before me.

"Really, lad," I winced at his complete lack of subtlety. "If you're going to listen in on conversations, you should at least *attempt* to be less obvious about it. Not to mention, Van Helsing has … far more important obligations to see to."

"No, m'lord, and a thousand apologies for the interruption," Remembering his place, Marius offered an abbreviated bow and salute. "Father Van Helsing is *here*, and he's gravely injured."

I moved in a blur, following the wafting scent of blood to a crumpled body lying in a heap by the castle gates. With one hand on his shoulder, and the other bracing the middle of his spine, I rolled the priest onto his back. Assaulted by the stench of burned flesh, I gasped. His eyes had been burned from their sockets, the letters DG branded onto his forehead.

"Dorian Gray." Blindly reaching out, Van Helsing caught the front of my shirt and clung to me. "He … came … for … your son."

Tendrils of black rage clouded the edges of my vision. "How did this happen?" I hissed around my lengthening fangs.

"Rau … was desperate to be … like *you*." Rolling to his side, the priest's body shivered, shock from his trauma setting in. "Dorian … told him he had a vampire that would do … whatever he asked. Said he had … a method that would overpower … any allegiance they held … to you."

"*Marius!*" At the mention of his name, he darted to my side. "Gently as you can, take Father Van Helsing up to a room. Treat his wounds with your blood, but *do not* make him drink. The only sacrament he has ever desired is that of Jesus. We will honor his wishes."

"Yes, m'lord." A dip of his chin, and Marius bent to collect the frail priest.

Moving quiet as a shadow, Renfield positioned himself at my elbow to silently await orders.

"Gather our best men," I growled, hands curling into fists of rage at my sides. "Follow Rau's scent wherever it leads. I want my son brought home, *now*. Then, we will do what I should have long ago, and *end* Dorian Gray."

Lost in my own trance of violent intent, I almost missed it at first. So much time had passed since I last heard its rumblings, I stopped listening for them. In fact, since giving myself over to The Dragon and salting the earth with its essence, it silenced itself to me—its humble slave. All that changed in that pivotal moment, when from the darkest recesses of my mind came the unmistakable reverberation of its satanic chuckle.

TWENTY-NINE

VINX

WEDDING DAY

Have you heard from Carter?" Staring at my reflection in the full-length mirror, I smoothed my hands over the midsection of my wedding dress, patiently waiting while Micah fastened the long row of pearl buttons up the back. Soft silvery-white fabric pleated into cap sleeves at my shoulders. Cascades of silk traveled the length of me, hinting at the curves beneath with modest grace. A lace ribbon embellished with diamonds and pearls cinched the gown at my waist.

Hands hovering between my shoulder blades, Mics paused to shoot me a dubious glance in the mirror. "Are you being ironic, or hoping for a miracle? Because from what I can tell endless training and hours of meditation have our boy no closer to perfecting his Jedi mind trick. For right now, we need to encourage him to keep his mouth shut. One slip up will *literally* cost him his life."

"I know," I murmured, adjusting one of the pearled bobby pins that arranged my hair into a mass of loose curls falling to one side.

Micah tugged at the bodice of my gown with a touch more force than necessary, demanding I meet her stare. "I'm serious, Vincenza. Whatever you think you need to hear from him, you need to let it—and him—go."

Wetting my lips, I shifted my gaze to my open-toe shoes. "I know. We need to keep our eye on the prize. Speaking of, did we ever get the RSVP back from Jeremy?"

As the only women within my bubble, Mics and Elodie landed the coveted roles as my bridesmaids. Micah had already wiggled into the classic black strapless dress chosen for her. It was belted at the middle with an onyx pearl sash.

"No, no word," Brow furrowing, Mics resumed her buttoning duties. "That doesn't mean he won't show. Either way, this wedding helps us spin the narrative and show the world that we aren't the monsters they think we are. We need that now more than ever."

Fueled by her words, I straightened my spine and tried to find myself in the reflection of the soon-to-be queen peering back at me. "Don't worry about me, coach. You've drilled the playbook into my head. I'm primed and ready to go."

Taking a step back, Micah eyed her completed task. "Good, because it's time." Seizing me by the shoulders, she spun me to face her. "Remember; meek and mild. You are the blushing bride completely enraptured by this man—this god—who is whisking you away to your happily ever after. Basically, you need to go full Markle."

I placed my hand over hers, and offered a comforting squeeze. "I've got this, Mics. Really. You don't have to worry. I will be a delicate flower that radiates innocence and virtue. Then, tonight, we'll lace a gallon of stag blood with rum and see how much we have to drink to achieve a buzz for even a fraction of a second. You know, like, true fuckin' ladies."

Tip of her tongue nervously fiddling with the gold hoop in her lip, Micah yanked me into a crushing hug. "I love you, Vinx," she muttered against my hair. "Whatever happens from here, I need you to know that."

"Hey," I pulled back, forcing a brave face I wasn't feeling, "none of that, now. You hear? If Jer shows up, the Court and magi are in place to keep Markus and Rutherford distracted long enough for us to get him to safety. They won't want any kind of trouble. None of us do. Not when we all know the entire world is watching. We got this, Mics. *Believe* that."

In a perfect world, that might even have been true.

THIRTY
VLAD

Sixteen torturous days.

That's how long it took my men to track down Rau.

All those agonizingly long hours dragged by without answers. I couldn't bring myself to eat. The mere thought of blood made my gut churn in angry knots. Sleep, that elusive mistress, escaped me. Chased away by thoughts I couldn't quiet. Every time my eyes drifted shut, images flashed behind my lids of Rau's body rotting in a shallow grave, or my precious boy forced into servitude under Dorian's domain. Extreme exhaustion brought on the bleeds. Keeping a handkerchief clutched in my fist, I dabbed at the inky black gore oozing from my ears. Even that physical anguish could not match the emotional turmoil of not knowing.

I thought nothing could be worse.

I was … so very wrong.

Knowledge crashed through my castle doors, bouncing them on their hinges.

Renfield and Marius dragged a nightmarish version of my son into the foyer, their words spiraling down my pit of despair.

"Found him in England, m'lord. Whoever sired him abandoned him there before he turned. I would wager that to be out of fear of your wrath."

"When he awoke, ravenous, he had no one to teach him of the delicacy required to feed without harm. He gave into his hunger, and lost himself to bloodlust."

So focused was I on searching for traces of my son in the beast before me, that I barely heard either of them. Fangs bared, he gnashed his teeth with frothy spit foaming on his lips. Head whipping from side to side, he searched for something—*anything*—to sink his teeth into. Dried blood caked his clothing. His pupils dilated with crazed desire.

"We will dry him out, and train him to the proper ways. It will be agonizing for him, but it will pass if—"

I held up one hand to halt Renfield's preparations. "Where did you find him?"

The two exchanged matching looks of compassionate hesitation.

"It should matter not, Lord," Marius's tone betrayed him by wavering. "The lad has been returned to you!"

In a blink, my eyes transformed into gleaming rubies of death and mayhem. "The blood on him smells young, and unsoiled by this world. You can tell me the truth, or I can drain you both and see for myself. The choice is yours."

Brow pinched with fright, Marius glanced to Renfield in search of guidance.

Squaring his shoulders, Renfield met my stare with the stony chill of hard fact. "The alley his sire deserted him in was right next to ..." to my extreme surprise, even my most steadfast soldier stumbled over the words. "Whoever it was, abandoned him in an alley beside ... an orphanage."

Ears ringing, my mind and body went numb. "How many?"

Renfield cast his stare to the floor, seemingly choking on the number. "All of them. Babies, children, and the nuns tending to them. He spared ... no one."

Slowly, I dragged my gaze to the frothing, writhing version of my boy. The innocent babe I watched grow from boy to man had vanished, replaced by yet another blood-crazed fiend.

This was what I did to him.

This was what I unleashed on the world.

Stumbling back, I turned and caught myself with a hand on the wall.

"Sire?" Marius called after me. "What shall we do with your son?"

"He's not my son," Pushing off the blockade of stone, I dragged leaden feet forward in a trudge toward the rear of the castle. "My son ... is dead."

Hope was lost.

No good remained in this world.

Not anymore.

Everything I fought for, everything I held dear ... was gone.

All that remained was the rash of death and violence I unleashed.

As I created it, perhaps with my death it could be contained.

In the farthest wing of the castle lay the Dracul mausoleum. When each new heir was born, a place was reserved for them amongst the marble tombs. My own, a floor level crypt along the outer perimeter, taunted me since the day I was able to read my own name carved into the stone plate mounted on it. Curling my fingers into the edge of the stone slab lid, I pried it open. The inside was a void of nothingness, a fitting prison to match my hollowed soul.

Stepping one foot inside, a voice intervened from the threshold. "M'lord? What can I do? How may I serve thee?" The quake in Renfield's tone matched that of a dejected child.

"Seal me away," I peered his way with great regret, hating myself more still for dragging a man of God into my condemning curse. "Bury this tomb deep, with a mountainous pile of stone on top. Let me die a slow death, haunted every day by all I have wrought. I pray that the vampire infliction will die with me, and your soul will be free from damnation."

' Lord Vlad, no! Our kind are still capable of good! Believe in us! Let s prove it to you! *Father, please!*"

Climbing inside, I slid the lid shut on Renfield's desperate pleas. I igited a blaze of demonic flame scorching its way across the land with ravenous intent. If I accomplished nothing else, let my absence snuf it out.

THIRTY-ONE

VINX

WEDDING DAY

W hen your *exquisite* maid of honor reaches the halfway point, the music will switch to *Canon in D*. That will be your cue to begin your promenade into wedded bliss. Oh! You need your flowers!" With a theatrical twirl, the wedding planner, Dot, retrieved my bouquet. Her hair was a coiffed lavender cloud that defied gravity. Sparkling pink gems bejeweled the cat-framed glasses slipping down her nose. Dot gasped in melodramatic awe, holding up the flowers as if wielding Excalibur. "Three flawless white roses set against olive branches as a symbol of the peace the Nosferatu people long for. It's simplistic perfection."

Cradling the blooms in both hands, she delicately passed them to me.

"Thank you," Unable to match her level of awe over ... *flowers*, I forced a tight smile that quickly morphed into a wince when my hand closed around the bouquet's handle. "Ow! *Shit*."

Face folding into a mask of horror, Dot snapped a handkerchief from her pocket quick enough to impress a matador, ready to protect my gown in an instant. "Oh, goodness! Was there a thorn? I've worked with this florist before, she usually takes such care!"

Shifting the flowers to my left hand, I inspected the bothersome wound. On the tip of my index finger, I watched the tiny pin prick heal closed. Turning the bouquet handle, I found the culprit. Hidden within the white silk ribbon decorating the flower stalks, protruded a tiny silver needle. At a casual glance it may have seemed one of the pearl-topped corsage pins holding the ribbon in place simply broke. I knew in an instant that wasn't the case. A burn began at the sight of the wound, scorching up my arm.

I didn't have to guess what it was.

My nostrils twitched at the alluring scent of Dot's musty, old lady blood.

Mouth filling with saliva, my fangs ached to stretch free.

Artificial sulfur.

Someone drugged me.

Chin to my chest, I fought to maintain a clear head with Dot's pulse beckoning to me. "Who ... else handled the ... flowers?"

Dot's fake lashes appeared three times larger behind her thick lenses. "I couldn't begin to say, darling. Are you displeased? Is there anything I could add, or take away to make them better suit your—"

"*No!*" I snapped, recoiling as she reached for them. "They're lovely. Just wondering ... who all I should thank for ... each aspect of the wedding?"

"Everyone from the caterers to Lord Draculesti himself have been through here. Are you okay, doll? You're suddenly pale and ... shiny." Pulling a makeup puff from ... *somewhere* behind her, Dot came at me ready to blot.

Wanting nothing more than latch onto her throat and drain her dry in a vicious flurry, I held up one finger to halt her. "Nope. We're going for a glowy look today. What's that? *Huh*, the music changed. Guess that's my cue."

Before Dot could argue further, I held my head high and began my long walk down the aisle. Truth be told, I couldn't say if the shift in music was my prompt or not. No one bothered to check if the bride actually knew *Canon in D* from *Gangnam Style*.

Which she did *not*.

All I wanted was space to remind myself that I wasn't fully vampire. That the differences in my genetic makeup made me strong enough to fight passed the pull of the artificial sulfur with my composure somewhat intact. Granted, a ballroom packed to capacity wasn't the *best* place to test that theory. But, escapism seeks the next distraction, not logical alternatives.

Each row of linen-draped chairs was filled, the balconies overhead packed with people. A fresh coat of deep Boudreaux-colored paint covered the soaring walls. Glowing candles lined every aisle in an enchanted path. Maybe it was the blinding hunger talking, but the combination warmed the room to the entrancing hue of fresh spilled blood.

As I floated down the aisle, the who's who of the world's elite beamed up at me. Jaw clenched to the point of pain, I forced myself to breathe in the sweet perfume of their mingling scents. It was freshly grilled hamburgers, grandma's fried chicken, and an expertly seared steak combined in a tempting fusion. Absolute carnivorous perfection.

Vlad, Carter, and Finn stood at the altar, patiently waiting to receive me. I wish I had some romantic soliloquy about how handsome they looked, or even a randy musing of which wore their tuxedo best.

To me, they were predators threatening my prey.

Blinking hard, I fought for focus. The chemical shouldn't have affected me so potently. Logically, it made no sense. Unless, you added in a new independent variable to the freak show experiment that was my life.

Vlad's blood.

Having it in my system must have made me more susceptible.

Fantastic.

As far as things you can catch from a guy goes, ravenous cannibalism was right up there at the top of the absolute worst list.

Bright side? This was basically a chemical reaction based on a contaminant in my blood stream. Like using a soap my skin was sensitive to, I simply needed to wait it out for the irritant to fade.

"Are you okay?" Vlad muttered, reaching for my hand to help me up the two steps to the altar.

Clamping my lips down on an involuntary growl, the most I could muster was a twitch of a nod. Hand placed in his, I hitched up the hem of my gown to take the needed steps up.

To my left, Elodie seized Micah's arm, her urgent whisper hitting my ears like a scream. "*Her eyes! Look at her eyes!*"

What she saw, I couldn't say. Judging by the way the officiant recoiled when I peered up at him from under my lashes, I'm guessing it fell far short of blushing bride.

Shaking off his bout of shock, he threw his age-spot covered hand out wide and let his voice boom to the cheap seats. "Dearly beloved, we are gathered together today to join Lord Vlad Tepes of House Draculesti with Vincenza Meredith Larow in matrimony."

The ballroom door creaked open, allowing in a last-minute straggler.

With them came an odd stench of spoiled meat and fungal earth.

Vincenza." The thunderous echo of Carter's voice, snapped my head up. "*I need you to listen to me, and know I only have your best interest at heart.*"

Fearing he slipped up and signed his own death warrant or was moments from objecting to our vows, I glanced to Vlad. His impassive expression showed no signs he heard anything at all.

Vinx, whatever you do," Once more Carter's voice resonated all around, coming from everywhere and nowhere simultaneously. "*Don't turn around.*"

Like any normal person told not to turn, the very first thing I did was ... *turn.* Glancing over my shoulder at our gaggle of guests, the world slowed to a crawl.

Following my stare, Vlad's handed tightened protectively around mine.

"No, Vinx, don't look."

Micah whimpered, her hand fluttering to her mouth.

"Vincenza, no!"

Finn and Elodie dropped fang, their arms bent and ready to strike.

"Please ... close your eyes. Stay with me."

Elodie explained Carter would master telepathy when he had something worth saying. How I wish I had been wise enough to listen.

The sharp clap of wingtip shoes connecting with the marble floor resonated through the cathedral. "The Kingdom of Heaven is at hand for those strong enough to defeat the devil's temptations!" The cadence of Markus's commanding timbre transported me back to the airplane hangar where I barely made it out alive.

Striding down the aisle, Markus's expertly styled hair bobbed with each step. An arrogant half-grin twisted back one corner of his weaselly mouth.

At his side—as always—stood his glorified henchman, Neil Rutherford. The candlelight gleamed off Rutherford's bald head, his expression set in a hateful scowl. His fingers twitched toward his pocket, hinting he came armed.

My fangs were pushing from the folds in my gumline when Thomas planted himself in front of me. Good arm raised to halt my advance, the voice that rumbled from his lips was not his own. *"There's a door behind the altar."* Desperation I had yet to understand advanced Carter's powers to new realms, his plea broadcasting through the bewildered triplet. *"I'm begging you, Vinx. Go. You don't want to see—"*

Compelled to discover the truth, I pushed Thomas aside and stepped down from the altar.

"Yet, here we all are! Invited into the devil's den. Then again, the invitation really wasn't for *me* was it?" Markus caught my stare with a sinister sneer and dragged my attention down to his right hand.

Don't look. Don't ... Carter's final plea trailed off as my chin tipped downward.

Camera's clicked all around.

Whirring video footage captured every moment of wedding guests along the aisle scrambling to get away from Markus's grisly offer.

My eyes were open.

Peering directly at it.

Still, it took my brain a beat to register the depth of depravity right in front of me.

An item—no bigger than a bowling ball—dripped with tar-black fluid. Markus held tight to it in a fist of ... sandy brown hair.

"It's a head!"

"Good Lord, he's carrying a severed head!"

Panicked shrieks filled the ballroom, guests trampling over each other to get to the nearest exit.

"Your brother wanted so badly to be here," Markus *tsk*ed, his tongue clucking against the roof of his mouth. "He often spoke of reconnecting with you. Unfortunately, as is true for all other manner of paranormal freaks, his mask of civility slipped off to the most *horrible* consequences."

Jeremy.

Was it yesterday, or a lifetime ago, we were fighting over bathroom time?

"*Guards!*" Vlad roared, appearing at my side in a ripple of air.

Of course, it *had* to be the magi that flanked the perimeter, hunting for the best way to eradicate the problem. We couldn't have vampires putting their hands on humans. Oh, no. *That* would be wrong. They could lock us in their basements, crack our chests open, and play the xylophone on our exposed rib cages. Still, one flash of fang and we were rabid dogs that needed to be put down.

Markus threw his arms out wide, the gore from Jeremy's neck stub splashing over the pews and aisle runner. "They brought you here to sell you a lie! To make you believe they are beings *capable* of love! Oh, and they do play their parts well! Jeremy, here, *pretended* to be against vampire equality. Then, he charged into a rally and attacked innocent humans unprovoked. His face is splashed all over the news, along with grisly details about the three lives he took before anyone could subdue him. *This* is the truth! *This* is reality! Not some fairytale they are cramming down your throats, to lure you into a false sense of security amongst ... *fangers.*"

"Get them out of here, at once!"

"Sire, as soon as we get the guests out, we can flank them and have them immobilized in under a minute."

"Make it so!"

Magi cut between the pews, inching closer in anticipation of their window to strike.

So many shouts.

So much panicked inaction.

That's all it was.

Cautious impotence.

"They aren't like us, and I can prove it." Swinging his arm back, Markus released the head on the upsurge. Like the bowling ball I originally thought it was, Jeremy's head rolled down the aisle, colliding with my foot in a muted *thump.*

Gradually, my stare drifted downward to all that was left of my brother. Whatever thread of control I managed to maintain ... snapped. Red haze clouding the edges of my vision, a threatening hiss bubbled from my chest.

I didn't drop fang.

Not this time.

Not for him.

A blur of speed landed me inches from Markus. Head tilted, I peered his way with vulturine interest.

"What are you going to do, little girl?" Markus taunted in a barely audible whisper. "Remember, the world is watching."

"Vincenza, please," Vlad implored, keeping his tone soft and measured. "I didn't believe our kind was *capable* of good. You and your friends showed me how wrong I was. Don't let him drive you to darkness. Trust me, *copil*, there is no coming back from that."

"No one is driving me to darkness," I murmured vacantly. "I'm already there."

Hand shooting out, I punched my fist into Markus's chest cavity. Fingers closing around the pulsing lump of flesh within, I ripped his heart out with the indifference of pulling the plug on an old staticky radio. A slick of blood coated my arm to the elbow, splattering over my designer gown.

While a flicker of life still remained, I let Markus watch with bulging eyes while I licked his blood from my fingers. As he folded to the floor in a lifeless heap, I cast his still beating heart aside like the trash it was.

"You undead bitch!" Going for the gun in the inside pocket of his suit coat, Rutherford charged.

Heightened reflexes made it easy to catch his elbow in midair. Pulling straight up, hard and fast, I yanked his shoulder from its socket with a sickening *thunk*. Anguished screams tearing from his throat, I silenced him by driving the heel of my palm into his nose. The cartilage jammed into his brain in a spray of gore.

The magi swarmed, moving in to stop me.

Let them try.

Let them all try.

I was eager to share my pain.

THIRTY-TWO
VLAD

WEDDING DAY

A life unhinged.

The binding rules of compliance severed.

Before any vampire could move to save Vincenza from herself, silver shackles appeared on our wrists and ankles. Air swirled in a crackle of magic, sewing the lips shut of all Nosferatu in the room, except for myself.

"Vlad, Vlad, Vlad," Dorian's voice in my ear sent shivers of hate pulsing down my spine. "This all could have been avoided, old friend. Had you simply been worthy of The Dragon from the start. Instead, you decided to take the clichéd dark and broody approach, whining over your soul's damnation. Really, watch a movie or six, that angle is *long* since played out."

I barely acknowledged him, stare fixated on my gore splattered bride lashing out at every Magi that dared come near her.

Lacing his fingers in front of him, Dorian cocked his head to consider me. "I'm surprised you didn't rush in, like the hero you believe yourself to be. Even before I clapped irons on you, there was a definite hesitation."

Rage plunged her dagger into Vinx's thigh, tearing muscle and fabric with its serrated edge. Grabbing her by the back collar of her robe, Vinx flung the petite magi at the wall in a flailing pinwheel.

"Who ... would I help in this equation?"

Dorian's mouth curved into a downward C. "Good point. Either way, it's safe to say your honeymoon is ruined. Tell me, how will you spin this? The would-be-queen taking human lives while the world watches? That's sure to be a PR nightmare. Forget vampire equality, humans will line up with silver and stakes to go to war with your kind after this."

Glancing to Vinx's friends, I found them looking every bit as helpless and mystified as I felt. Even their skin blistering and cracking beneath the scorching shackles couldn't tear their attention from the horror unfolding.

"I honestly don't know," I managed, wincing as Ego sprinted straight for Vincenza, only to be flipped over her shoulder and spiked to the ground.

"There's still *one* way." Dorian wrung his hands with a mischievous grin. "I have no desire for The Dragon myself. With my powers and immortality, I feel such servitude would be a bit too ... *confining* for my taste. However, I would love to find a more *worthy* playmate. One who will help me usher in the war I've longed for. After all, I've taunted and goaded you in countless unspeakable ways, and still you sought the *noble* way out," his nose crinkled in disgust at the word. "Truth be told, it's maddening. That said, I'll make you a deal. Let me try once more to lure The Dragon out of you, to place it in the receptacle of my choosing. I was going to use Markus. Unfortunately, it seems his *heart* wasn't in the task. Horrible joke, had to be made. Back to the point. Give me what I want, and I'll work my magic to make all this unpleasantness go away. I have the original footage of what happened in that airplane hangar, *and* vials of the artificial sulfur in my possession. We could blow this story wide open, paint a picture of your wife as a victim in an unfortunate manipulation scheme. For good measure, I can even guarantee your adorable little NPI Bill is passed by the end of the week. What do you say?"

"No."

Tendons in his neck bulging, Dorian's face morphed from red to purple. "You stubborn bastard. You've *lost*! You have no other options! You were never worthy of The Dragon's gift! Always rolling over, and showing your soft underbelly the instant someone you cared for was harmed! A true adversary draws strength from loss. Look at *her*." His hand stabbed in Vincenza's direction. "Barely more than a child, yet her pain molded her into a true specimen of destruction. Why? *Why won't you part with what was never meant to be yours?*"

"Because," tone vacant of emotion, I spoke over his indignant rant, "The Dragon ... is no longer inside of me. Where he roosted for so long remains only the gaping hole of his absence. He reduced me to just another body to be counted amongst the vampire bloodline."

Dorian's mouth swung open and shut. "Wha ... ? *How?* How is that possible?"

After elbowing Greed in the solar plexus, Vincenza curled one arm around his throat and snapped his neck. "It would seem, *Drákon* deemed *another* worthy. You said it yourself, she is a true specimen of destruction."

Dorian followed my stare, watching with fresh interest as the last magi fell by Vinx's hand. Her arms hung limp at her sides, hands still curled into vicious claws. Chin drooping to her chest, fat drops of blood dripped from her hair. Once the pinnacle of elegant fashion, her white gown was shredded to ribbons and stained with crimson gore.

"This puny little nobody? The Dragon has accomplished nothing more than finding itself another *slave*." Lip curling in disgust, Dorian rolled one wrist, intending to disappear in a magical fog.

Vincenza moved with the force of a raging storm cloud. Arms and legs morphing into tendrils of black mist, she seized Dorian by the throat and held him there until he was forced corporeal.

"You're the one who molested my mind." Pressing in, intimately close, she breathed the words into him. "The puppet master that set all of this up. It had to be you, because Markus believed Jeremy was a vampire. We both know he was actually reanimated by a necromancer. The same one *you* forced me to kill for you, to tie up that little loose end."

"Look at you following the breadcrumbs." Pupils dilating with desire, Dorian pulled his chin back enough to allow his lecherous gaze to travel the length of my bride. "The new slave to the darkness. *Mmm.* I'm inclined to take back my previous reservations. You'll do *quite* nicely."

Vincenza added to her ghoulish appearance by dropping fang. Tilting her head, she raked the tips of her incisors over Dorian's throat. "This isn't going to go the way you think it is. I tried the civilized approach, and your lackeys brought me my brother's *head.* I suggest you take that little painting of yours, and hide it away. Because I'm coming for you, Dorian, and anyone else that gets in my way."

"Such fire and flare. It's absolutely delicious. Makes me want to beg you to make it hurt so good. Sadly, you're only role in this is as the arm candy coating." One onyx brow hitched in interest, Dorian searched Vincenza's face for traces of the beast within. "I seek ... your new master."

I knew the truth before she uttered it.

I felt it in the throbbing energy radiating off of her.

What I lived in fear of for so long, she conquered with reckless abandon.

A malevolent smile teased at the corners of Vincenza's full lips. "That's where you're wrong. I have no master. The darkness *did* speak to me. While I stood barefoot on the blood-soaked floor—surrounded by my fresh kills—it stretched and roiled from the shadows around me. With breath reeking of fire and brimstone, it praised my fortitude and bowed to my strength." Stepping back, she threw her arms out wide, owning her title. "In that moment, it called me ... *Queen*."

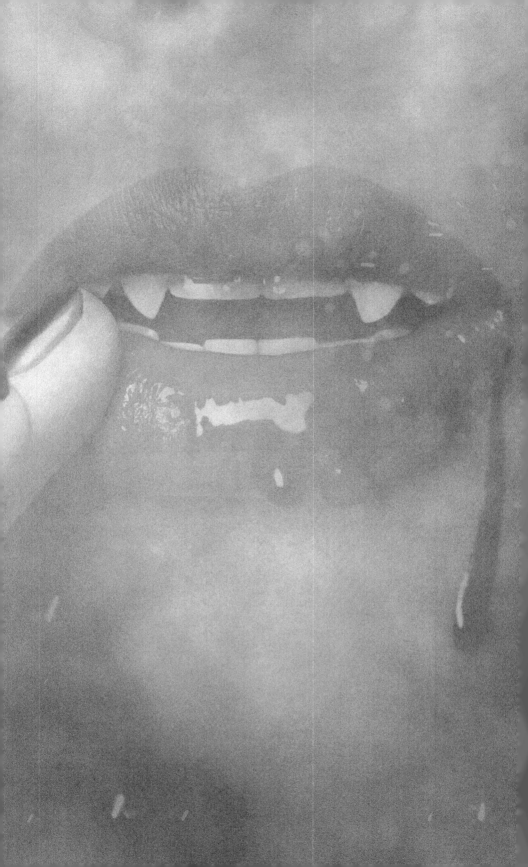

The Veiled Series
continues with Vendetta, coming soon!

ABOUT THE AUTHOR

Stacey Rourke is the author of award-winning books that span various genres, yet maintain her trademark blend of action and humor. She lives in Florida with her husband, two beautiful daughters, and two giant dogs. She loves to travel, has an unhealthy shoe addiction, and considers herself blessed to make a career out of talking to the imaginary people that live in her head.

Connect with her at:

www.staceyrourke.com

Facebook at www.facebook.com/staceyrourkeauthor

or on Twitter or Instagram @rourkewrites

Sign up for her newsletter at: http://eepurl.com/c56flr

TS901 CHRONICLES (CO-WRITTEN WITH TISH THAWER)

T2901: Anomaly
TS901: Dominion

ARCHIVE OF THE FIVES:

Apocalypse Five

THE JOURNALS OF OCTAVIA HOLLOWS:

How the Dead Lie (A Havenwood Falls Novella)
Wake the Dead

Made in the USA
Las Vegas, NV
05 May 2022